BOOKS BY

Donald Barthelme

SNOW WHITE   *1967*

COME BACK, DR. CALIGARI   *1964*

SNOW WHITE

Donald Barthelme

SNOW WHITE

Atheneum New York

ATHENEUM
Macmillan Publishing Company
866 Third Avenue, New York, NY 10022
Collier Macmillan Canada, Inc.

Library of Congress catalog card number 67-14324
ISBN 0-689-70331-7

Macmillan books are available at special discounts for bulk purchases
for sales promotions, premiums, fund-raising, or educational use.
For details, contact:

Special Sales Director
Macmillan Publishing Company
866 Third Avenue
New York, NY 10022

20   19   18   17   16   15   14

First Atheneum Paperback Printing 1972

Printed in the United States of America

This book first appeared, in slightly different form,
in THE NEW YORKER. Certain portions also appeared,
in different form, in HARPER'S BAZAAR and PARIS REVIEW.

for Birgit

PART ONE

SHE is a tall dark beauty containing a great many beauty spots: one above the breast, one above the belly, one above the knee, one above the ankle, one above the buttock, one on the back of the neck. All of these are on the left side, more or less in a row, as you go up and down:

       o

       o

       o

       o

       o

       o

The hair is black as ebony, the skin white as snow.

BILL is tired of Snow White now. But he cannot tell her. No, that would not be the way. Bill can't bear to be touched. That is new too. To have anyone touch him is unbearable. Not just Snow White but also Kevin, Edward, Hubert, Henry, Clem or Dan. That is a peculiar aspect of Bill, the leader. We speculate that he doesn't want to be involved in human situations any more. A withdrawal. Withdrawal is one of the four modes of dealing with anxiety. We speculate that his reluctance to be touched springs from that. Dan does not go along with the anxiety theory. Dan does not believe in anxiety. Dan speculates that Bill's reluctance to be touched is a physical manifestation of a metaphysical condition that is not anxiety. But he is the only one who speculates that. The rest of us support anxiety. Bill has let us know in subtle ways that he doesn't want to be touched. If he falls down, you are not to pick him up. If someone holds out a hand in greeting, Bill smiles. If it is time to wash the buildings, he will pick up his own bucket. Don't hand him a bucket, for in that circumstance there is a chance that your hands will touch. Bill is tired of Snow White. She must have noticed that he doesn't go to the shower room, now. We are sure she has noticed that. But Bill has not told her in so many words that he is tired of her. He has not had the heart to unfold those cruel words, we speculate. Those cruel words remain locked in his lack of heart. Snow White must assume that his absence from the shower room, in these days, is an aspect of his not liking to be touched. We are certain she has assumed that. But to what does she attribute the "not-liking" itself? We don't know.

"OH I wish there were some words in the world that were not the words I always hear!" Snow White exclaimed loudly. We regarded each other sitting around the breakfast table with its big cardboard boxes of "Fear," "Chix," and "Rats." Words in the world that were not the words she always heard? What words could those be? "Fish slime," Howard said, but he was a visitor, and rather crude too, and we instantly regretted that we had lent him a sleeping bag, and took it away from him, and took away his bowl too, and the Chix that were in it, and the milk on top of the Chix, and his spoon and napkin and chair, and began pelting him with boxes, to indicate that his welcome had been used up. We soon got rid of him. But the problem remained. What words were those? "Now we have been left sucking the mop again," Kevin said, but Kevin is easily discouraged. "Injunctions!" Bill said, and when he said that we were glad he was still our leader, although some of us had been wondering about him lately. "Murder and create!" Henry said, and that was weak, but we applauded, and Snow White said, "That is one I've never heard before ever," and that gave us courage, and we all began to say things, things that were more or less satisfactory, or at least adequate, to serve the purpose, for the time being. The whole thing was papered over, for the time being, and didn't break out into the open. If it had broken out into the open, then we would really have been left sucking the mop in a big way, that Monday.

THEN we went out to wash the buildings. Clean buildings fill your eyes with sunlight, and your heart with the idea that man is perfectible. Also they are good places to look at girls from, those high, swaying wooden platforms: you get a rare view, gazing at the tops of their red and gold and plum-colored heads. Viewed from above they are like targets, the plum-colored head the center of the target, the wavy navy skirt the bold circumference. The white or black legs flopping out in front are like someone waving his arms over the top of the target and calling, "You missed the center by not allowing sufficiently for the wind!" We are very much tempted to shoot our arrows into them, those targets. You know what that means. But we also pay attention to the buildings, gray and noble in their false architecture and cladding. There are Tip-arillos in our faces and heavy jangling belts around our waists, and water in our buckets and squeegees on our poles. And we have our beer bottles up there too, and drink beer for a second breakfast, even though that is against the law, but we are so high up, no one can be sure. It's too bad Hogo de Ber-gerac isn't up here with us, because maybe the experience would be good for him, would make him less loathsome. But he would probably just seize the occasion to perform some new loathsome act. He would probably just throw beer cans down into the street, to make irritating lumps under the feet of those girls who, right this minute, are trying to find the right typewriter, in the correct building.

NOW she's written a dirty great poem four pages long, won't let us read it, refuses absolutely, she is adamant. We discovered it by accident. We had trudged home early, lingered in the vestibule for a bit wondering if we should trudge inside. A strange prehension, a boding of some kind. Then we trudged inside. "Here's the mail," we said. She was writing something, we could see that. "Here's the mail," we said again, usually she likes to paw over the mail, but she was preoccupied, didn't look up, not a flicker. "What are you doing there," we asked, "writing something?" Snow White looked up. "Yes," she said. And looked down again, not a pinch of emotion coloring the jet black of her jet-black eyes. "A letter?" we asked wondering if a letter then to whom and about what. "No," she said. "A list?" we asked inspecting her white face for a hint of *tendresse*. But there was no *tendresse*. "No," she said. We noticed then that she had switched the tulips from the green bowl to the blue bowl. "What then?" we asked. We noticed that she had shifted the lilies from the escritoire to the chiffonier. "What then?" we repeated. We observed that she had hauled the Indian paintbrush all the way out into the kitchen. "Poem," she said. We had the mail in our paws still. "Poem?" we said. "Poem," she said. There it was, the red meat on the rug. "Well," we said, "can we have a peek?" "No," she said. "How long is it?" we asked. "Four pages," she said, "at present." "*Four pages!*" The thought of this immense work . . .

Vacillations and confusions of Snow White: "But who am I to love?" Snow White asked hesitating, because she already loved us, in a way, but it wasn't enough. Still, she was slightly ashamed.

THEN I took off my shirt and called Paul, because we were planning to break into his apartment, and if he was there, we could not do so. If he was there we would be recognized, he would know who we were, and that we were carrying his typewriter out into the street to sell it. He would know everything about us: how we made our living, what girls we liked, where we kept the vats. Paul didn't answer so it wasn't necessary to ask if Anna was there—the prepared name we were going to ask for. Paul sat in his baff, under the falling water. He was writing a palinode. "Perhaps it is wrong to have favorites among the forms," he reflected. "But retraction has a special allure for me. I would wish to retract everything, if I could, so that the whole written world would be . . ." More hot water fell into the baff. "I would retract the green sea, and the brown fish in it, and I would especially retract that long black hair hanging from that window, that I saw today on my way here, from the Unemployment Office. It has made me terribly nervous, that hair. It was beautiful, I admit it. Long black hair of such texture, fineness, is not easily come by. Hair black as ebony! Yet it has made me terribly nervous. Why some innocent person might come along, and see it, and conceive it his duty to climb up, and discern the reason it is being hung out of that window. There is probably some girl attached to it, at the top, and with her responsibilities of various sorts . . . teeth . . . piano lessons. . . . There is the telephone ringing, now. Who is it? Who or what wants me? I will not answer. That way, I am safe, for the time being."

THERE is a river of girls and women in our streets. There are so many that the cars are forced to use the sidewalks. The women walk in the street proper, the part where, in other cities, trucks and bicycles are found. They stand in windows too unbuckling their shirts, so that we will not be displeased. I admire them for that. We have voted again and again, and I think they like that, that we vote so much. We voted to try the river in the next town. They have a girl-river there they don't use much. We slipped into the felucca carrying our baggage in long canvas tubes tied, in the middle, with straps. The girls groaned under the additional weight. Then Hubert pushed off and Bill began to beat time for the rowers. We wondered if Snow White would be happy, alone there. But if she wasn't, we couldn't do anything about it. Men try to please their mistresses when they, men, are not busy in the countinghouse, or drinking healths, or having the blade of a new dagger chased with gold. In the village we walked around the well where the girls were dipping their trousers. The zippers were rusting. "Ha ha," the girls said, "we could tear this down in a minute, this well." It is difficult to defeat that notion, the one the village girls hold, that the boy who trembles by the wall, against the stones, will be Pope someday. He is not even hungry; his family is not even poor.

WHAT is Snow White thinking? No one knows. Today she came into the kitchen and asked for a glass of water. Henry gave her a glass of water. "Aren't you going to ask me what I want this glass of water for?" she asked. "I assumed you wanted to drink it," Henry said. "No, Henry," Snow White said. "Thirsty I am not. You are not paying attention, Henry. Your eye is not on the ball." "What do you want the glass of water for, Snow White?" "Let a hundred flowers bloom," Snow White said. Then she left the room, carrying the glass of water. Kevin came in. "Snow White smiled at me in the hall," Kevin said. "Shut up Kevin. Shut up and tell me what this means: *let a hundred flowers bloom.*" "I don't know what it means Henry," Kevin said. "It's Chinese, I know that." What is Snow White thinking? No one knows. Now she has taken to wearing heavy blue bulky shapeless quilted People's Volunteers trousers rather than the tight tremendous how-the-West-was-won trousers she formerly wore, which we admired immoderately. An unmistakable affront I would say. We are getting pretty damned sick of the whole thing, of her air of being just about to do something and of the dozen-odd red flags and bugles she has nailed to the dining-room table. We are getting pretty damned sick of the whole thing and our equanimity is leaking away and finding those tiny Chairman Mao poems in the baby food isn't helping one bit, I can tell you that.

THE PSYCHOLOGY OF SNOW WHITE:

IN THE AREA OF FEARS, SHE FEARS

MIRRORS

APPLES

POISONED COMBS

IN addition to washing the buildings, we make baby food, Chinese baby food:

BABY BOW YEE (*chopped pork and Chinese vegetables*)

BABY DOW SHEW (*bean curd stuffed with ground pike*)

BABY JAR HAR (*shrimp in batter*)

BABY GOOK SHAR SHEW BOW (*sweet roast pork*)

BABY PIE GUAT (*pork and oysters in soy sauce*)

BABY GAI GOON (*chicken, bean sprouts and cabbage*)

BABY DIM SUM (*ground pork and Chinese vegetables*)

BABY JING SHAR SHEW BOW (*sweet roast pork and apples*)

That is how we spend our time, tending the vats. Although sometimes we spend our time washing the buildings. The vats and the buildings have made us rich. It is amazing how many mothers will spring for an attractively packaged jar of Baby Dim Sum, a tasty-looking potlet of Baby Jing Shar Shew Bow. Heigh-ho. The recipes came from our father. "Try to be a man about whom nothing is known," our father said, when we were young. Our father said several other interesting things, but we have forgotten what they were. "Keep quiet," he said. That we remember. He wanted more quiet. One tends to want that, in a National Park. Our father was a man about whom nothing was known. Nothing is known about him still. He gave us the recipes. He was not very interesting. A tree is more interesting. A suitcase is more interesting. A canned good is more interesting. When we sing the father hymn, we notice that he was not very interesting. The words of the hymn notice it. It is explicitly commented upon, in the text.

"I UNDERSTAND all this about Bill," Henry said. He had unlocked the locks on the bar and we were all drinking. "Nevertheless I think somebody ought to build a fire under him. He needs a good kick in the back according to my way of thinking. Couldn't we give him a book to read that would get him started. It bothers me to come in at night and see him sitting there playing Hearts or something, all that potential being pissed away. We are little children compared to him, in terms of possibility, and yet all he seems to want to do is sit around the game room, and shuffle the Bezique cards, and throw darts and that sort of thing, when he could be out realizing his potential. We are like little balls of dust under his feet, potentially, and he merely sits there making ships inside bottles, and doing scrimshaw, and all that, when he could be out maximizing his possibilities. Boy I would like to build a fire under that boy. I'll be damned if I know what to do about this situation which is vexing me in a hundred ways. It's just such a damned shame and crime I can't stand it, the more I think about it. I just want to go out and hurl boxes in the river, the more I think about it, and rage against fate, that one so obviously chosen to be the darling of the life-principle should be so indolent, impious and wrong. I am just about at the end of my tether, boys, and I'll say that to his face, too!"

20

AT dinner we discussed the psychiatrist. "And the psychiatrist?" we said. "He was unforgivable," she said. "Unforgivable?" "He said I was uninteresting." "Uninteresting?" "He said I was a screaming bore." "He should not have said that." "He said he wasn't in this for the money." "For what then?" "He was in this for grins, he said." "The expression is unfamiliar." "There were not a million grins in my history, he said." "That was shabby of him." "He said let's go to a movie for God's sake." "And?" "We went to a movie." "Which?" "A Charlton Heston." "How was it?" "Excellent." "Who paid?" "He." "Was there popcorn?" "Mars Bars." "Did you hold hands?" "*Naturellement.*" "And after?" "Drinks." "And after that?" "Don't pry." "But," we said putting down the duck, "*three days* at the psychiatrist's . . ." We regarded Snow White, her smooth lips and face, her womanly figure swaying there, at the window. Something was certainly wrong, we felt. "Most life is unextraordinary," Clem said to Snow White, in the kitchen. "Yes," Snow White said, "I know. Most life is unextraordinary looked at with a woman's desperate eye too it might interest you to know." Dan keeps telling Snow White that "Christmas is coming!" How can he be killed most easily? With the fewest stains?

THE pretty airline stewardess regarded Clem's chest through his transparent wash-and-wear nylon shirt. "He has that sort of fallen-in chest many boys from the West have, as if a cow had fallen on him, in his early life. Only one shirt. The shirt on his back. How appealing that is! Surely I must do something for this poor Westerner!" In the rear baggage compartment Clem sweated over the ironing board Carol had made out of a pile of old suitcases. "Snow White waits for me," Clem reflected while ironing his shirt. "Although she also waits for Bill, Hubert, Henry, Edward, Kevin and Dan, I cannot help feeling that, when everything is said and done, she is essentially mine. Even though I am aware that each of the others feels the same way." Clem replaced the iron in the bucket. His shirt looked fine now, just fine. The aircraft landed softly, just as it should. The stairway fell correctly onto the landing strip. The passengers followed protocol in getting off, the most famous emerging first, the most ignoble emerging last. Clem was in the lower middle. He regarded the Volkswagens crowding the Chicago streets, the children freaking out in their Army surplus, the black grime falling from the sky. "So this is the Free World! I would so like to make 'love' in a bed, just once. Making it in the shower is fine, on ordinary days, but on one's vacation there should be something a little different, it seems to me. A bed would be a sensational novelty. I suppose I must seek out a bordel. I assume they can be found in the Yellow Pages. It is not Snow White that I would be being unfaithful to, but the shower. Only a collection of white porcelain and shiny metal, at bottom."

THE SECOND GENERATION OF ENG-
LISH ROMANTICS INHERITED THE
PROBLEMS OF THE FIRST, BUT COM-
PLICATED BY THE EVILS OF INDUSTRI-
ALISM AND POLITICAL REPRESSION.
ULTIMATELY THEY FOUND AN AN-
SWER NOT IN SOCIETY BUT IN VARI-
OUS FORMS OF INDEPENDENCE FROM
SOCIETY:

HEROISM

ART

SPIRITUAL TRANSCENDENCE

BEAVER COLLEGE is where she got her education. She studied *Modern Woman, Her Privileges and Responsibilities:* the nature and nurture of women and what they stand for, in evolution and in history, including householding, upbringing, peace-keeping, healing and devotion, and how these contribute to the rehumanizing of today's world. Then she studied *Classical Guitar I*, utilizing the methods and techniques of Sor, Tarrega, Segovia, etc. Then she studied *English Romantic Poets II:* Shelley, Byron, Keats. Then she studied *Theoretical Foundations of Psychology:* mind, consciousness, unconscious mind, personality, the self, interpersonal relations, psychosexual norms, social games, groups, adjustment, conflict, authority, individuation, integration and mental health. Then she studied *Oil Painting I* bringing to the first class as instructed Cadmium Yellow Light, Cadmium Yellow Medium, Cadmium Red Light, Alizarin Crimson, Ultramarine Blue, Cobalt Blue, Viridian, Ivory Black, Raw Umber, Yellow Ochre, Burnt Sienna, White. Then she studied *Personal Resources I and II:* self-evaluation, developing the courage to respond to the environment, opening and using the mind, individual experience, training, the use of time, mature redefinition of goals, action projects. Then she studied *Realism and Idealism in the Contemporary*

Italian Novel: Palazzeschi, Brancati, Bilenchi, Pratolini, Moravia, Pavese, Levi, Silone, Berto, Cassola, Ginzburg, Malaparte, Mapalarte, Calvino, Gadda, Bassani, Landolfi. Then she studied—

"I AM princely," Paul reflected in his eat-in kitchen. "There is that. At times, when I am 'down,' I am able to pump myself up again by thinking about my blood. It is blue, the bluest this fading world has known probably. At times I startle myself with a gesture so royal, so full of light, that I wonder where it comes from. It comes from my father, Paul XVII, a most kingly man and personage. Even though his sole accomplishment during his long lack of reign was the de-deification of his own person. He fluttered the dovecotes with that gesture, when he presented himself as mortal and just like everybody else. A lot of people were surprised. But the one thing they could not take away from him, there in that hall bedroom in Montreaux, was his blood. And the other thing they could not take away from him was his airs and graces, which I have inherited, to a sickening degree. Even at fifty-five he was still putting cologne in his shoes. But I am more experimental than he was, and at the same time, more withdrawn. The height of his ambition was to tumble the odd chambermaid now and then, whereas I have loftier ambitions, only I don't know what they are, exactly. Probably I should go out and effect a liaison with some beauty who needs me, and save her, and ride away with her flung over the pommel of my palfrey, I believe I have that right.

But on the other hand, this duck-with-blue-cheese sandwich that I am eating is mighty attractive and absorbing, too. He was peculiar, my father. That much can safely be said. He knew some things that other men do not know. He heard the swans singing just before death, and the bees barking in the night. That is what he said, but I didn't believe him, then. Now, I don't know."

HENRY was noting his weaknesses on a pad. Process comparable to searching a dog's underbelly for fleas. The weaknesses pinched out of the soul's ecstasy one by one. Of course "ecstasy" is being used here in a very special sense, as misery, something that would be in German one of three aspects of something called the *Lumpwelt* in some such sentence as, "The *Inmitten*-ness of the *Lumpwelt* is a turning toward misery." So that what is meant here by ecstasy is something on the order of "fit," but a kind of slow one, perhaps a semi-arrested one, and one that is divisible by three. "Should I go to Acadia and remove my parents from there? From that parking place where they have been parked since 1936? It is true that they are well connected to the ground now, with gas and water lines and geraniums. The uprooting would be considerable. The fear of the father's frown. That deters me. He is happy there, as far as I know; still I have this feeling that he ought to be rescued. From that natural beauty." Then Dan came in. "Dan, what is an interrupted screw?" Henry asked. "An interrupted screw," Dan said, "is a screw with a discontinuous helix, as in a cannon breech, formed by cutting away part or parts of the thread, and sometimes part of the shaft. Used with a lock nut having corresponding male sections." "This filthy,"

Henry said, "this language thinking and stinking everlastingly of sex, screw, breech, 'part,' shaft, nut, male, it is no wonder we are all going round the bend with this language dinning forever into our eyes and ears. . . ." "I am not going round the bed," Dan said, "not me." "Round the *bend*," Henry said, "the bend not the bed, how is it that I said 'bend' and you heard 'bed,' you see what I mean, it's inescapable." "You live in a world of your own Henry." "I can certainly improve on what was given," Henry said.

"THOSE men   hulking   hulk in closets and
outside   gestures eventuating against a white
screen difficulties   intelligence   I only wanted
one plain hero of incredible size and soft, flexible
manners   parts   thought   dissembling
limb   add up the thumbprints on my shoulders
    Seven is too   moves too much and is absent
partly   different levels of emotional release cal-
culated paroxysms   scug   dissolve thinking
parts of faces   lower area of Clem from the nose's
bottom to the line, an inch from the chin cliff
not enough ever   Extra difficulty! His use of
color!   Firmness   mirror   custody of the
blow   scale model   I concede that it is
to a degree   instruments   adequate distances
parched   to touch each one with invisible kindly
general delivery hands, washing motions   mirror
    To take turns and then say "Thank you"
congress of eyes turning with a firm, soft glance
up   Edward never   extra density of the
blanched product rolling   tongue   child
straight ahead   broken exterior facing   natural gas   To experience a definition placed neatly
where you can't reach it and higher up   Day-
time experiences   choler   film bliss"

JANE replaced the Hermes Rocket on the shelf. Another letter completed. That made twenty-five letters completed. Only eighteen more letters to complete. She had tried to make them irritating in the extreme. She reread the last letter. She was trembling. It was irritating in the extreme. Jane stopped trembling. There was Hogo to think about, now, and Jane preferred to think about Hogo without trembling. "He knows when I tremble. That is what he likes best." Hogo drove Jane down Meat Street in his cobra-green Pontiac convertible. Nobody likes Hogo, because he is loathsome. He always has a white dog sitting upright in the front seat of the car, when Jane is not sitting there. Jane likes to swing from the lianas that dangle from the Meat Street trees, so sometimes she is not sitting there and the dog is sitting there instead. "For God's sake can't you stay put?" "Sorry." Jane fingered her amulet. "That *canaille* Hogo. If he wants an exotic girl like me then he has to put up with a few irregularities from time to time." Hogo is not very simpatico—not much! He changed his name to Hogo from Roy and he wears an Iron Cross t-shirt and we suspect him of some sort of shady underground connection with Paul—we haven't figured out exactly what yet. "Hogo can I have an ice cream—a chocolate swirl?" Hogo took the chocolate swirl and jammed it into Jane's mouth, in a loathsome way. His mother loved him when he was Roy, but now that he is Hogo she won't even speak to him, if she can help it.

"IT is marvelous," Snow White said to herself. "When the water falls on my tender back. The white meat there. Give me the needle spray. First the hot, and then the cold. A thousand tiny points of perturbation. More perturbation! And who is it with me, here in the shower? It is Clem. The approach is Clem's, and the technique, or lack of it, is Clem, Clem, Clem. And Hubert waits outside, on the other side of the shower curtain, and Henry in the hall, before the closed door, and Edward is sitting downstairs, in front of the television, waiting. But what of Bill? Why is it that Bill, the leader, has not tapped at my shower-stall door, in recent weeks? Probably because of his new reluctance to be touched. That must be it. Clem you are downright anti-erotic, in those blue jeans and chaps! Artificial insemination would be more interesting. And why are there no in-flight movies in shower stalls, as there are in commercial aircraft? Why can't I watch Ignace Paderewski in *Moonlight Sonata*, through a fine mist? That was a picture. And he was president of Poland, too. That must have been interesting. Everything in life is interesting except Clem's idea of sexual congress, his Western confusion between the concept, 'pleasure,' and the concept, 'increasing the size of the herd.' But the water on my back is interesting. It is more than interesting. Marvelous is the word for it."

34

THERE were some straw flowers there. Decor. And somebody had said something we hadn't heard, but Dan was very excited. "I praise fruit and hold flowers in disdain," Apollinaire said, and we contrasted that with what LaGuardia had said. Then Bill said something: "Torch in the face." He was very drunk. Other people said other things. I smoked an Old Gold cigarette. It is always better when everybody is calm, but calm does not come every day. Lamps are calm. The Secretary of State is calm. Each day just goes so fast, begins and ends. The poignant part came when Edward began to say what everybody already knew about him. "After I read the book, I—" "Don't say that Edward," Kevin said. "Don't say anything you'll regret later." Bill put a big black bandage over Edward's mouth, and Clem took off all his clothes. I smoked an Old Gold cigarette, the same one I had been smoking before. There was still some of it left because I had put it down without finishing it. Alicia showed us her pornographic pastry. Some things aren't poignant at all and that pornographic pastry is one of them. Bill was trying to keep the tiredness off his face. I wanted to get out of this talk and look at the window. But Bill had something else to say, and he wasn't going to leave until he had said it, I could see that. "Well it is a pleasure to please her, when human ingenuity can manage it, but the whole thing is just trembling on the edge of monotony, after several years. And yet . . . I am fond of her. Yes, I am. For when sexual pleasure is had, it makes you fond, in a strange way, of the other one, the one with whom you are having it."

SNOW WHITE was cleaning. "Book lice do not bite people," she said to herself. She sprayed the books with a five-percent solution of DDT. Then she dusted them with the dusting brush of the vacuum cleaner. She did not bang the books together, for that injures the bindings. Then she oiled the bindings with neat's-foot oil, applying the oil with the palm of her hand and with her fingers. Then she mended some torn pages using strips cut from rice paper. She ironed some rumpled pages with a warm iron. Fresh molds were wiped off the bindings with a clean soft cloth slightly dampened with sherry. Then she hung a bag containing paradichlorobenzene in the book case, to inhibit mildew. Then Snow White cleaned the gas range. She removed the pans beneath the burners and grates and washed them thoroughly in hot suds. Then she rinsed them in clear water and dried them with paper towels. Using washing soda and a stiff brush, she cleaned the burners, paying particular attention to the gas orifices, through which the gas flows. She cleaned out the ports with a hairpin, rinsed them thoroughly and dried them with paper towels. Then she returned the drip tray, the burners and grates to their proper positions and lit each burner to make sure it was working. Then she washed the inside of the broiler compartment with a cloth wrung out in warm suds, with just a bit of ammonia to help cut the grease. Then she rinsed the broiler compartment with a cloth wrung out in clear water and dried it with paper towels. The pan and rack of the broiler were done in the same way. Then Snow White cleaned the oven using steel wool on the tough spots. Then she rinsed the inside of the oven with a cloth wrung out in clear water and dried it with paper towels. Then, "piano care."

WHAT SNOW WHITE REMEMBERS:

THE HUNTSMAN

THE FOREST

THE STEAMING KNIFE

"I WAS fair once," Jane said. "I was the fairest of them all. Men came from miles around simply to be in my power. But those days are gone. Those better days. Now I cultivate my malice. It is a cultivated malice, not the pale natural malice we knew, when the world was young. I grow more witchlike as the hazy days imperceptibly meld into one another, and the musky months sink into memory as into a slough, sump, or slime. But I have my malice. I have that. I have even invented new varieties of malice, that men have not seen before now. Were it not for the fact that I am the sleepie of Hogo de Bergerac, I would be *total malice*. But I am redeemed by this hopeless love, which places me along the human continuum, still. Even Hogo is, I think, chiefly enamored of my malice, that artful, richly formed and softly poisonous network of growths. He luxuriates in the pain potential I am surrounded by. I think I will just sit here on this porch swing, now, swinging gently in the moist morning, and remember 'better days.' Then a cup of Chinese-restaurant tea at 10 a.m. Then, back into the swing for more 'better days.' Yes, that would be a pleasant way to spend the forenoon."

AT the horror show Hubert put his hand in Snow White's lap. A shy and tentative gesture. She let it lay there. It was warm there; that is where the vulva is. And we had brought a thermos of glittering Gibsons, to make us happy insofar as possible. Hubert remembered the Trout Amandine he had had the day the ball was sticking to Kevin's leg. It had been extremely tasty, that trout. And Hubert remembered the conversation in which he had said that God was cruel, and someone else had said vague, and they had pulled the horse off the road, and then they had seen a Polish picture. But this picture was better than that one, allowing for the fact that we had experienced that one in translation, and not in the naked Polish. Snow White is agitated. She is worried about something called her "reputation." What will people think, why have we allowed her to become a public scandal, we must not be seen in public *en famille*, no one believes that she is simply a housekeeper, etc. etc. These concerns are ludicrous. No one cares. When she is informed that our establishment has excited no special interest in the neighborhood, she is bitterly disappointed. She sulks in her room, reading Teilhard de Chardin and thinking. "My suffering is authentic enough but it has a kind of low-grade concrete-block quality. The seven of them only add up to the equivalent of about two *real men*, as we know them from the films and from our childhood, when there were giants on the earth. It is possible of course that there are no more *real men* here, on this ball of half-truths, the earth. That would be a disappointment. One would have to content oneself with the subtle falsity of color films of unhappy love affairs, made in France, with a Mozart score. That would be difficult."

Miseries and complaints of Snow White: "I am tired of being just a horsewife!"

DEAR MR. QUISTGAARD:

Although you do not know me my name is Jane. I have seized your name from the telephone book in an attempt to enmesh you in my concerns. We suffer today I believe from a lack of connection with each other. That is common knowledge, so common in fact, that it may not even be true. It may be that we are overconnected, for all I know. However I am acting on the first assumption, that we are underconnected, and thus have flung you these lines, which you may grasp or let fall as you will. But I feel that if you neglect them, you will suffer for it. That is merely my private opinion. No police power supports it. I have no means of punishing you, Mr. Quistgaard, for not listening, for having a closed heart. There is no punishment for that, in our society. Not yet. But to the point. You and I, Mr. Quistgaard, are not in the same universe of discourse. You may not have been aware of it previously, but the fact of the matter is, that we are not. We exist in different universes of discourse. Now it may have appeared to you, prior to your receipt of this letter, that the universe of discourse in which you existed, and puttered about, was in all ways adequate and satisfactory. It may never have crossed your mind to think that other universes of discourse distinct from your own existed, with people in them, discoursing. You may have, in a commonsense way, regarded your own u. of d. as a plenum, filled to the brim with discourse. You may have felt that what already existed was a sufficiency. People like you often do. That is certainly one way of regarding it, if fat self-satisfied complacency is your aim. But I say unto you, Mr. Quistgaard, that even a plenum can leak. Even a plenum, *cher maître*, can be penetrated. New things can rush into your plenum displacing old things, things that were formerly there. No man's plenum, Mr. Quistgaard, is impervious to the awl of God's will. Consider then your situation *now*. You are sitting there in your house on Neat Street, with your fine dog, doubtless, and your handsome wife and tall brown sons, conceivably, and who knows with your gun-colored Plymouth Fury in the driveway, and opinions passing back and forth, about whether the Grange should build a new meeting hall or not, whether the children should become Thomists or not, whether the pump needs more cup grease or not. A comfortable American scene. *But I, Jane Villiers de l'Isle-Adam, am in possession of your telephone number, Mr. Quistgaard.* Think what that means. It means that at any moment I can pierce your plenum with a single telephone call, simply by dialing 989–7777. You are correct, Mr. Quistgaard, in seeing this as a threatening situation.

The moment I inject discourse from my u. of d. into your u. of d., the yourness of yours is diluted. The more I inject, the more you dilute. Soon you will be presiding over an empty plenum, or rather, since that is a contradiction in terms, over a former plenum, in terms of yourness. You are, essentially, in my power. I suggest an unlisted number.

Yours faithfully,
JANE

PAUL: A FRIEND OF THE FAMILY

"IS there someplace I can put this?" Paul asked indicating the large parcel he held in his arms. "It is a new thing I just finished today, still a little wet I'm afraid." He wiped his hands which were covered with emulsions on his trousers. "I'll just lean it up against your wall for a moment." Paul leaned the new thing up against our wall for a moment. The new thing, a dirty great banality in white, poor-white and off-white, leaned up against the wall. "Interesting," we said. "It's poor," Snow White said. "Poor, poor." "Yes," Paul said, "one of my poorer things I think." "Not so poor of course as yesterday's, poorer on the other hand than some," she said. "Yes," Paul said, "it has some of the qualities of poorness." "Especially poor in the lower left-hand corner," she said. "Yes," Paul said, "I would go so far as to hurl it into the marketplace." "They're getting poorer," she said. "Poorer and poorer," Paul said with satisfaction, "descending to unexplored depths of poorness where no human intelligence has ever been." "I find it extremely interesting as a social phenomenon," Snow White said, "to note that during the height of what is variously called, abstract expressionism, action painting and so forth, when most artists were grouped together in a school, you have persisted in an image alone. That, I find—and I think it has been described as hard-edge painting, is an apt description, although it leaves out a lot, but I find it very interesting that in the last few years there is a tremendous new surge of work being done in the hard-edge image. I don't know if you want to comment on that, but I find it extremely interesting that you, who have always been sure of yourself and your image, were one of the earliest, almost founders of that school, if you can even call it a school." "I have always been sure of myself and my image," Paul said. "Sublimely poor," she murmured. "Wallpaper," he said. They kissed. We trudged to bed then singing the to-bed song heigh-ho. She was lying there in her black vinyl pajamas. "He is certainly a well-integrated personality, Paul," she said. "Yes," we said. "He makes contact, you must grant him that." "Yes," we said. "A beautiful human being." "Carrying the mace is a bit much, perhaps," we said. "We are fortunate to have him in our country," she concluded.

THEN we went over to Paul's place and took the typewriter. Then the problem was to find somebody to sell it to. It was a fine Olivetti 22, that typewriter, and the typewriter girls put it under their skirts. Then George wanted to write something on it while it was under their skirts. I think he just wanted to get under there, because he likes Amelia's legs. He is always looking at them and patting them and thrusting his hand between them. "What are you going to write under there, George?" "I thought perhaps some automatic writing, because one can't see so well under here with the light being strangled by the thick wool, and I touch-type well enough, but I can't see to think, so I thought that . . ." "Well we can't sell this typewriter if you're typing on it under Amelia's legs, so come out of there. And bring the carbon paper too because the carbon paper makes black smudges on Amelia's legs and she doesn't want that. Not now." We all had our hands on the typewriter when it emerged because it had been in that pure grotto, Paul's place, and tomorrow we are going to go there again and take the elevator cage this time, so that he can't come down into the street any more, with his pretensions.

"YES," Bill said, "I wanted to be great, once. But the moon for that was not in my sky, then. I had hoped to make a powerful statement. But there was no wind, no weeping. I had hoped to make a powerful statement, coupled with a moving plea. But there was no weeping, except, perhaps, concealed weeping. Perhaps they wept in the evenings, after dinner, in the family room, among the family, each in his own chair, weeping. A certain diffidence still clings to these matters. You laughed, sitting in your chair with your purple plywood spectacles, your iced tea. I had hoped to make a significant contribution. But they remained stony-faced. Did I make a mistake, selecting Bridgeport? I had hoped to bring about a heightened awareness. I saw their smiling faces. They were going gaily to the grocery for peanut oil, Band-Aids, Saran Wrap. My census of tears was still incomplete. Why had I selected Bridgeport, city of concealed meaning? In Calais they weep openly, on street corners, under trees, in the banks. I wanted to provide a definitive account. But my lecture was not a success. Men came to fold the folding chairs, although I was still speaking. You laughed. I should talk about things people were interested in, you said. I wanted to achieve a breakthrough. My penetrating study was to have been a masterly evocation, sobs and cries, these things matter. I had in mind initiating a multi-faceted program involving paper towels and tears. I came into the room suddenly, you were weeping. You slipped something out of sight, under the pillow.

" 'What is under the pillow?' I asked.

" 'Nothing,' you said.

"I reached under the pillow with my hand. You grasped my wrist. An alarm clock spread the alarm. I rose to go. My survey of the incidence of weeping in the bedrooms of members of the faculty of the University of Bridgeport was methodologically sound but informed, you said, by too little compassion. You laughed, in your room, pulling from under the pillow grainy gray photographs in albums, pictures of people weeping. I wanted to effect a *rapprochement*, I wanted to reconcile irreconcilable forces. What is the reward for knowing the worst? The reward for knowing the worst is an honorary degree from the University of Bridgeport, salt tears in a little bottle. I wanted to engage in a meaningful dialogue, but the seminal thinkers I contacted were all shaken with sobs, wracked is the word for it. Why did we conceal that emotion which, had we declared it, could have liberated us? There are no parameters for measuring the importance of this question. My life-enhancing poem was mildly meretricious, as you predicted. I wanted to substantiate an unsubstantiated report, I listened to the Blue Network, I heard weeping. I wanted to make suitable arrangements but those whose lives I had thought to arrange did not appear on the appointed day. They were deployed elsewhere marching and counter-marching on fields leased from the Police Athletic League. I was perhaps not lucky enough. I wanted to make a far-reaching reevaluation. I had in mind launching a three-pronged assault, but the prongs wandered off seduced by fires and clowns. It was hell there, in the furnace of my ambition. It was because, you said, I had read the wrong book. He reversed himself in his last years, you said, in the books no one would publish. But his students remember, you said."

THE REVOLUTION OF THE PAST GEN-
ERATION IN THE RELIGIOUS SCIENCES
HAS SCARCELY PENETRATED POPU-
LAR CONSCIOUSNESS AND HAS YET
TO SIGNIFICANTLY INFLUENCE PUB-
LIC ATTITUDES THAT REST UPON TO-
TALLY OUTMODED CONCEPTIONS.

PAUL sat in his baff, wondering what to do next. "Well, what shall I do next? What is the next thing demanded of me by history?" If you know who it is they are whispering about, then you usually don't like it. If Paul wants to become a monk, that's his affair entirely. Of course we had hoped that he would take up his sword as part of the President's war on poetry. The time is ripe for that. The root causes of poetry have been studied and studied. And now that we know that pockets of poetry still exist in our great country, especially in the large urban centers, we ought to be able to wash it out totally in one generation, if we put our backs into it. But we were prepared to hide our disappointment. The decision is Paul's finally. "Are those broken veins in my left cheek, above the cheekbone there? No, thank God, they are only tiny whiskers not yet whisked away. Missed in yesterday's scrape, but vulnerable to the scrape of today." Besides, most people are not very well informed about the cloistered life. Certainly they can have light bulbs if they want them, and their rivers and mountains are not inferior to our own. "They make interesting jam," Hank said. "But it's his choice, in the final analysis. Anyhow, we have his typewriter. That much of him is ours, now." People were caressing each other under Paul's window. "Why are all these people existing under my window? It is as if they were as palpable as me—as bloody, as firm, as well-read." Monkish business will carry him to town sometimes; perhaps we will be able to see him then.

"MOTHER can I go over to Hogo's and play?"
"No Jane Hogo is not the right type of young man
for you to play with. He is thirty-five now and that
is too old for innocent play. I am afraid he knows
some kind of play that is not innocent, and will
want you to play it with him, and then you will
agree in your ignorance, and then the fat will be in
the fire. That is the way I have the situation figured
out anyhow. That is my reading of it. That is the
way it looks from where I stand." "Mother all this
false humility does not become you any more than
that mucky old poor little match-girl dress you are
wearing." "This dress I'll have you know cost two
hundred and forty dollars when it was new."
"When was it new?" "It was new in 1918, the year
your father and I were in the trenches together, in
the Great War. That was a war all right. Oh I
know there have been other wars since, better-
publicized ones, more expensive ones perhaps, but
our war is the one I'll always remember. Our war is
the one that means *war* to me." "Mother I know
Hogo is thirty-five and thoroughly bad through
and through but still there is something drawing me
to him. To his house. To the uninnocence I know
awaits me there." "Simmer down child. There is a
method in my meanness. By refusing to allow you
to go to Hogo's house, I will draw Hogo here, to

your house, where we can smother him in blueberry *flan* and other kindnesses, and generally work on him, and beat the life out of him, in one way or another." "That's shrewd mother."

THE poem remained between us like an immense, wrecked railroad car. "Touching the poem," we said, "is it rhymed or free?" "Free," Snow White said, "free, free, free." "And the theme?" "One of the great themes," she said, "that is all I can reveal at this time." "Could you tell us the first word?" "The first word," she said, "is 'bandaged and wounded.'" "But . . ." "Run together," she said. We mentally reviewed the great themes in the light of the word or words, "bandaged and wounded." "How is it that bandage precedes wound?" "A metaphor of the self armoring itself against the gaze of The Other." "The theme is loss, we take it." "What," she said, "else?" "Are you specific as to what is lost?" "Brutally." "Snow White," we said, "why do you remain with us? here? in this house?" There was a silence. Then she said: "It must be laid, I suppose, to a failure of the imagination. I have not been able to imagine anything better." *I have not been able to imagine anything better.* We were pleased by this powerful statement of our essential mutuality, which can never be sundered or torn, or broken apart, dissipated, diluted, corrupted or finally severed, not even by art in its manifold and dreadful guises. "But my imagination is stirring," Snow White said. "Like the long-sleeping stock certificate suddenly alive in its green safety-deposit box because of new investor interest, my imagination is stirring. Be warned." Something was certainly wrong, we felt.

THE HORSEWIFE IN HISTORY

FAMOUS HORSEWIVES

THE HORSEWIFE: A SPIRITUAL PORTRAIT

THE HORSEWIFE: A CRITICAL STUDY

FIRST MOP, 4000 BC

VIEWS OF ST. AUGUSTINE

VIEWS OF THE VENERABLE BEDE

EMERSON ON THE AMERICAN HORSEWIFE

OXFORD COMPANION TO THE AMERICAN
HORSEWIFE

INTRODUCTION OF BON AMI, 1892

HORSEWIVES ON HORSEWIFERY

ACCEPT ROLE, PSYCHOLOGIST URGES

THE PLASTIC BAG

THE GARLIC PRESS

BILL has developed a shamble. The consequence, some say, of a lost mind. But that is not true. In the midst of so much that is true, it is refreshing to shamble across something that is not true. He does not want to be touched. But he is entitled to an idiosyncrasy. He has earned it by his vigorous leadership in that great enterprise, his life. And in that other great enterprise, our love for Snow White. "This thing is damaging to all of us," Bill noted. "We were all born in National Parks. Clem has his memories of Yosemite, inspiring gorges. Kevin remembers the Great Smokies. Henry has his Acadian songs and dances, Dan his burns from Hot Springs. Hubert has climbed the giant Sequoias, and Edward has climbed stately Rainier. And I, I know the Everglades, which everybody knows. These common experiences have yoked us together forever under the red, white and blue." Then we summoned up all our human understanding, from those regions where it customarily dwelt. "Love has died here, apparently," Bill said significantly, "and it is our task to infuse it once again with the hot orange breath of life. With that in mind I have asked Hogo de Bergerac to come over and advise us on what should be done. He knows the deaths of the heart, Hogo does. And he knows the terror of aloneness, and the rot of propinquity, and the absence of grace. He should be here tomorrow. He will be wearing blueberry *flan* on his buttonhole. That is how we are to know him. That and his vileness."

HOGO was reading a book of atrocity stories. "God, what filthy beasts we were," he thought, "then. What a thing it must have been to be a Hun! A filthy Boche! And then to turn around and be a Nazi! A gray vermin! And today? We co-exist, we co-exist. Filthy deutschmarks! That so eclipse the very mark and texture . . . That so eclipse the very mark and bosom of a man, that vileness herself is vilely o'erthrown. That so enfold . . . That so enscrap . . . Bloody deutschmarks! that so enwrap the very warp and texture of a man, that what we cherished in him, vileness, is . . . Dies, his ginger o'erthrown. Bald pelf! that so ingurgitates the very wrack and mixture of a man, that in him the sweet stings of vileness are, all ginger fled, he . . ." Henry walked home with his suit in a plastic bag. He had been washing the buildings. But something was stirring in him, a wrinkle in the groin. He was carrying his bucket too, and his ropes. But the wrinkle in his groin was monstrous. "Now it is necessary to court her, and win her, and put on this clean suit, and cut my various nails, and drink something that will kill the millions of germs in my mouth, and say something flattering, and be witty and bonny, and hale and kinky, and pay her a thousand dollars, all just to ease this wrinkle in the groin. It seems a high price." Henry let his mind stray to his groin. Then he let his mind stray to her groin. Do girls have groins? The wrinkle was still there. "The remedy of Origen. That is still open to one. That door, at least, has not been shut."

KEVIN was being "understanding." We spend a lot of our time doing that. And even more of our time, now that we have these problems. "Yes that's the way it is Clem," Kevin said to his friend Clem. "That's the way it is. You tell it like it is Clem baby." Kevin said a lot more garbage to Clem. Peacocks walked through the yard in their gold suits. "Sometimes I see signs on walls saying *Kill the Rich*," Clem said. "And sometimes *Kill the Rich* has been crossed out and *Harm the Rich* written underneath. A clear gain for civilization I would say. And then the one that says *Jean-Paul Sartre Is a Fartre*. Something going on there, you must admit. Dim flicker of something. On the other hand I myself have impulses toward violence uneasily concealed. Especially when I look out of the window at the men and women walking there. I see a great many couples, men and women, walking along in the course of a day because I spend so much time, as we all do, looking out of windows to determine what is out there, and what should be done about it. Oh it is killing me the way they walk down the street together, laughing and talking, those men and women. Pushing the pram too, whether the man is doing it, or the woman is doing it. Normal life. And a fine October chill in the air. It is unbearable, this consensus, this damned felicity. When I see a couple fighting I give them a dollar, because fighting is interesting. Thank God for fighting." "That's true Roger," Kevin said a hundred times. Then he was covered with embarrassment. "No I mean that's true Clem. Excuse me. Roger is somebody else. You're not Roger. You're Clem. That's true, Clem." More peacocks walked through the yard in their splendid plumage.

WE opened eggs to let the yellow out. Bill was worried about the white part, but we told him not to worry about that. "People do it every day," Edward said. The giant meringue rose to the ceiling. We were all in it. Dan turned off the television set. "You can't cook according to what that woman says. She never has the proportions right, and I don't think there ought to be cannabis in this meringue anyhow." "I just don't like your world," Snow White said. "A world in which such things can happen." We gave her the yellows, but she still wasn't satisfied. It's easy enough to motivate policemen if you give them votes and scooters to ride about on, but soldiers are a little more difficult. More soldiers. Cash their checks. Just because they are soldiers is no reason for not cashing their checks. Philippe laid down his M-16, his M-21, his M-2 and his fully automatic M-9. Then he laid down his M-10 and his M-34 with its mouthfed adapter. Then he laid down his M-4 and his M-3. It made a pile, that hardware. "Well I suppose that identifies you," the girl behind the wall said. Then she gave him his money, and gave the other men their money too. We were amazed that the performance was allowed to continue. There were a lot of things against the government in it. We gave Snow White the yellows in an aluminum container.

But she still wasn't satisfied. That is the essential point here, that she wasn't satisfied. I don't know what to do next.

The psychology of Snow White: What does she hope for? "Someday my prince will come." By this Snow White means that she lives her own being as incomplete, pending the arrival of one who will "complete" her. That is, she lives her own being as "not-with" (even though she is in some sense "with" the seven men, Bill, Kevin, Clem, Hubert, Henry, Edward and Dan). But the "not-with" is experienced as stronger, more real, at this particular instant in time, than the "being-with." The incompleteness is an ache capable of subduing all other data presented by consciousness. I don't go along with those theories of historical necessity, which suggest that her actions are dictated by "forces" outside of the individual. That doesn't sound reasonable, in this case. *Irruption of the magical in the life of Snow White:* Snow White knows a singing bone. The singing bone has told her various stories which have left her troubled and confused: of a bear transformed into a king's son, of an immense treasure at the bottom of a brook, of a crystal casket in which there is a cap that makes the wearer invisible. This must not continue. The behavior of the bone is unacceptable. The bone must be persuaded to confine itself to events and effects susceptible of confirmation by the instrumentarium of the physical sciences. Someone must reason with the bone.

"I AM being followed by a nun in a black station wagon." Bill wiped his hands on the seat covers. "I cannot fall apart now. Not yet. I must hold the whole thing together. Everything depends on me. I must conceal my wounds, contrive to appear unwounded. They must not know. The bloody handkerchief stuffed under the shirt. Now she signals a right turn. Now I will make a left turn. That way I shall escape her. But she makes a left turn too. There it is. That does it. She is following me. Following the spiritual spoor of my invisible wounds. Is she the great black horse for which I have waited all my days, since I was twelve years old? The great devouring black horse? Of course not. Don't be ridiculous, Bill. You are behaving like a fool. She is nothing like a black horse. She is simply a woman in a black dress, in a black station wagon. That she signals for a right turn and then makes a left turn means nothing at all. Don't think about it. Think about leadership. No, don't think about leadership. If you hang a right at this corner . . . No, she hung a right too. Don't think about it. Don't think. Turn on the radio. Think about what the radio is telling you. Think about the various messages to be found there."

I'm not her cup of tea I'm afraid
Ah ah ah ah ah
I'll find a way somehow in my lonely room
Ah ah ah ah ah
Emily Dickinson, why have you left me and gone
Ah ah ah ah ah
*Emily Dickinson, don't you know what we could
    have meant*
Ah ah ah ah ah

"HELLO Hogo." "Hello chaps." "The floor is yours Hogo." "Well chaps first I'd like to say a few vile things more or less at random, not only because it is expected of me but also because I enjoy it. One of them is that this cunt you've got here, although I've never seen her with my own eyes, is probably not worth worrying about. Now excuse me if I'm treading on your toes in this matter. God knows I love a female gesture as much as any man, as when, for instance, sitting in the front seat of a car in their bikini, they kind of shrug themselves into a street shift before getting out, or while the car door is open but they haven't gotten out yet; and if you happen to be looking out of a window of a house near the curb, or if you can move your window nearer the curb, you can sometimes see one sitting in her absolute underwear, in the hot weather, and then going through that 'shrugging' business, and sort of hitching the shift up over her hips, and then shaking her head to get the hair to fall the right way, and all that. And all this is the best that has been thought and said, in my opinion, or ever will be thought and said, for the only thing worth a rap in the whole world is the beauty of women, and maybe certain foods, and possibly music of all kinds, especially 'cheap' music such as that furnished at parades by for instance the St. Pulaski Tatterdemalion Band of Orange, New Jersey, which can reduce you to tears, in the right light, by speaking to you from the heart about your land, and what a fine land it is, and that it is *your* land really, and my land, this land of ours—that particular insight can chill you, rendered by a marching unit. But I wander. The main thing I wanted to point out is that the world is full of cunts, that they grow like clams in all quarters of the earth, cunts as multitudinous as cherrystones and littlenecks burrowing into the mud in all the bays of the world. The point is that the loss of any particular one is not to be taken seriously. She stays with you as long as she can put up with your shit and you stay with her as long as you can put up with her shit. That's the way it is behind the veil of flummery that usually veils these matters. Now think, I ask you, of all those women who are beyond the moment of splendor. They are depressed. The minister comes to call and recommends to them the things of the spirit, and tells them how the things of the spirit are more durable than the things of the flesh and all that. Well he is entirely correct, they are more durable, but durable is not what we wanted. The terrible poignance of this predicament is not vitiated by the fact that everybody knows it, in the backs of their minds. Ruin of the physical envelope is our great theme here, and if we keep changing girls every four or five years, it is because of this ruin, which I will never agree to, to my dying day. And that is why I keep looking out of the window, and why we all keep looking out of the window, to see what is passing, what has been cast up on the beach of our existence. Because something is always being cast up on that beach, as new classes of girls mature, and you can always get a new one, if you are willing to overlook certain weaknesses in the departments of thought and feeling. But if it is thought and feeling you want, you can always read a book, or see a film, or have an interior monologue. But of course with the spread of literacy you now tend to get girls who have thought and feeling too, in some measure, and some of them will probably belong to the Royal Philological Society or something, or in any case have their own 'thing,' which must be respected, and catered to, and nattered about, just as if you gave a shit about all this *blague*. But of course we may be different, perhaps you do care about it. It's not unheard of. But my main point is that you should bear in mind multiplicity, and forget about uniqueness. The earth is broad, and flat, and deep, and high. And remember what Freud said."

THE VALUE THE MIND SETS ON
EROTIC NEEDS INSTANTLY SINKS AS
SOON AS SATISFACTION BECOMES
READILY AVAILABLE. SOME OBSTACLE
IS NECESSARY TO SWELL THE TIDE
OF THE LIBIDO TO ITS HEIGHT, AND
AT ALL PERIODS OF HISTORY, WHEN-
EVER NATURAL BARRIERS HAVE NOT
SUFFICED, MEN HAVE ERECTED CON-
VENTIONAL ONES.

"*Which prince?*" Snow White wondered brushing her teeth. "Which prince will come? Will it be Prince Andrey? Prince Igor? Prince Alf? Prince Alphonso? Prince Malcolm? Prince Donalbain? Prince Fernando? Prince Siegfried? Prince Philip? Prince Albert? Prince Paul? Prince Akihito? Prince Rainier? Prince Porus? Prince Myshkin? Prince Rupert? Prince Pericles? Prince Karl? Prince Clarence? Prince George? Prince Hal? Prince John? Prince Mamillius? Prince Florizel? Prince Kropotkin? Prince Humphrey? Prince Charlie? Prince Matchabelli? Prince Escalus? Prince Valiant? Prince Fortinbras?" Then Snow White pulled herself together. "Well it is terrific to be anticipating a prince —to be waiting and knowing that what you are waiting for is a prince, packed with grace—but it is still waiting, and waiting as a mode of existence is, as Brack has noted, a darksome mode. I would rather be doing a hundred other things. But slash me if I will let it, this waiting, bring down my lofty feelings of anticipation from the bedroom ceiling where they dance overhead like so many French letters filled with lifting gas. I wonder if he will have the Hapsburg Lip?"

PAUL stood before a fence posing. He was on his way to the monastery. But first he was posing in front of a fence. The fence was covered with birds. Their problem, in many ways a paradigm of our own, was "to fly." "The engaging and wholly charming way I stand in front of this fence here," Paul said to himself, "will soon persuade someone to discover me. Then I will not have to go to the monastery. Then I can be on television or something, instead of going to the monastery. Yet there is no denying it, something is pulling me toward that monastery located in a remote part of Western Nevada." Lanky, generous-hearted Paul! "If I had been born well prior to 1900, I could have ridden with Pershing against Pancho Villa. Alternatively, I could have ridden with Villa against the landowners and corrupt government officials of the time. In either case, I would have had a horse. How little opportunity there is for young men to have personally owned horses in the bottom half of the twentieth century! A wonder that we U.S. youth can still fork a saddle at all. . . . Of course there are those 'horses' under the hoods of Buicks and Pontiacs, the kind so many of my countrymen favor. But those 'horses' are not for me. They take the tan out of my cheeks and the lank out of my arms and legs. Tom Lea or Pete Hurd will never paint me

standing by this fence if I am sitting inside an El-
dorado, Starfire, Riviera or Mustang, no matter
how attractively the metal has been bent."

SNOW WHITE let down her hair black as ebony from the window. It was Monday. The hair flew out of the window. "I could fly a kite with this hair it is so long. The wind would carry the kite up into the blue, and there would be the red of the kite against the blue of the blue, together with my hair black as ebony, floating there. That seems desirable. This motif, the long hair streaming from the high window, is a very ancient one I believe, found in many cultures, in various forms. Now I recapitulate it, for the astonishment of the vulgar and the refreshment of my venereal life."

THE President looked out of his window. He was not very happy. "I worry about Bill, Hubert, Henry, Kevin, Edward, Clem, Dan and their lover, Snow White. I sense that all is not well with them. Now, looking out over this green lawn, and these fine rosebushes, and into the night and the yellow buildings, and the falling Dow-Jones index and the screams of the poor, I am concerned. I have many important things to worry about, but I worry about Bill and the boys too. Because I am the President. Finally. The President of the whole fucking country. And they are Americans, Bill, Hubert, Henry, Kevin, Edward, Clem, Dan and Snow White. They are Americans. My Americans."

QUESTIONS:

1. Do you like the story so far? Yes ( ) No ( )
2. Does Snow White resemble the Snow White you remember? Yes ( ) No ( )
3. Have you understood, in reading to this point, that Paul is the prince-figure? Yes ( ) No ( )
4. That Jane is the wicked stepmother-figure? Yes ( ) No ( )
5. In the further development of the story, would you like more emotion ( ) or less emotion ( )?
6. Is there too much *blague* in the narration? ( ) Not enough *blague?* ( )
7. Do you feel that the creation of new modes of hysteria is a viable undertaking for the artist of today? Yes ( ) No ( )
8. Would you like a war? Yes ( ) No ( )
9. Has the work, for you, a metaphysical dimension? Yes ( ) No ( )
10. What is it (twenty-five words or less)?_____

_____

_____

_____

_____

_____

11. Are the seven men, in your view, adequately characterized as individuals? Yes ( ) No ( )
12. Do you feel that the Authors Guild has been sufficiently vigorous in representing writers before the Congress in matters pertaining to copyright legislation? Yes ( ) No ( )
13. Holding in mind all works of fiction since the War, in all languages, how would you rate the present work, on a scale of one to ten, so far? (Please circle your answer)

    1   2   3   4   5   6   7   8   9   10
14. Do you stand up when you read? ( ) Lie down? ( ) Sit? ( )
15. In your opinion, should human beings have more shoulders? ( ) Two sets of shoulders? ( ) Three? ( )

PART TWO

PERHAPS we should not be sitting here tending the vats and washing the buildings and carrying the money to the vault once a week, like everybody else. Perhaps we should be doing something else entirely, with our lives. God knows what. We do what we do without thinking. One tends the vats and washes the buildings and carries the money to the vault and never stops for a moment to consider that the whole process may be despicable. Someone standing somewhere despising us. In the hot springs of Dax, a gouty thinker thinking, father forgive them. It was worse before. That is something that can safely be said. It was worse before we found Snow White wandering in the forest. Before we found Snow White wandering in the forest we lived lives stuffed with equanimity. There was equanimity for all. We washed the buildings, tended the vats, wended our way to the county cathouse once a week (heigh-ho). Like everybody else. We were simple bourgeois. We knew what to do. When we found Snow White wandering in the forest, hungry and distraught, we said: "Would you like something to eat?" Now we do not know what to do. Snow White has added a dimension of confusion and misery to our lives. Whereas once we were simple bourgeois who knew what to do, now we are complex bourgeois who are at a loss. We do not like this complexity. We circle it wearily, prodding it from time to time with a shopkeeper's forefinger: What is it? Is it, perhaps, *bad for business?* Equanimity has leaked away. There was a moment, however, when equanimity was not the chief consideration. That moment in which we looked at Snow White and understood for the first time that we were fond of her. That was a moment.

Reaction to the hair: Two older men standing there observed Snow White's hair black as ebony tumbling from the window. "Seems like some hair comin' outa that winda there," one said. "Yes it looks like hair to me," his companion replied. "Seems like there oughta be somethin' to be done about it." "Yes, seems like it oughta be punished with a kiss or something." "Well we're too old for all that. You need a Paul or Paul-figure for that sort of activity. Probably Paul is even now standing in the wings, girding his pants for his entrance. So I guess I'll go along to the hiring hall, where I hear there might be some work." "I'll go along with you," the other man said, "because even though I ain't a A.B., I *am* a B.A., and maybe in the dimness the one thing will be taken for the other, and we can 'ship out' together." "I hate to go away and leave all that hair hanging there unmolested as it were," the first man said, "but we have a duty to our families, and to the country's merchant fleet, some vessels of which are now languishing at their berths doubtless, down at Pier 27 and Pier 32, for the lack o' the likes of us. So farewell, hair! Fare thee well, and if forever, still forever, fare thee well!"

Reaction to the hair: Fred the rock-and-roll band-leader addressed his men. "Men, something happened to me today on Monument Street. I saw a wall of hair black as ebony falling from a high window. A girl, a look . . . Men, everything is changed. I am changed. I am no longer the Fred of former times. And I say that things must be different with you, too, because you are my men, and I am your leader. Now it is quite clear to me that you men wish to play the buffalo music of your forefathers rather than the rock-and-roll we have patented, amplified, advertised and been paid for. Now I want to say right now, that that's all right with me, the buffalo music I mean. From this day forward, until the end of time, it will be nothing but buffalo music, in all the dromes of the world. I don't care a rap, that's how all right it is with me, this freedom that I freely grant you, that our gray hides have been hankering for. Now that, with a look, this mysterious dark beauty has changed my life, which *needed* to be changed, we are, in a strange way, opened to ourselves, and to buffalo music, until the red slag of the nooisphere descends to cover everything with the salty finality of love. So go forth now with your amplifiers and all, and revise your lives upward, as I have revised mine. Put the question mercilessly: Where have the buffalo gone?" Fred's men exchanged silent looks. "It's always like this," the looks said, "in the spring. It's always this way, when the green comes again. Our leader suffers a spiritual regeneration, from a bad man into a good man. It's always some girl, who looks at him, at which he falls into her power absolutely. We are tired of having for a leader one who is nothing else than a damned fool. Let's go down to the union hall, now, and write out the specifications for a grievance against him, under Section Four, the grievance section, of our union constitution. And we can think of other things, too, to add to the list of charges. That will be amusing, writing out the charges."

Reaction to the hair: "Well, that is certainly a lot of hair hanging there," Bill reflected. "And it seems to be hanging from our windows too. I mean, those windows where the hair is hanging are in our house, surely? Now who amongst us has that much hair, black as ebony? I am only pretending to ask myself this question. The distasteful answer is already known to me, as is the significance of this act, this hanging, as well as the sexual meaning of hair itself, on which Wurst has written. I don't mean that he has written *on* the hair, but rather about it, from prehistory to the present time. There can be only one answer. It is Snow White. It is Snow White who has taken this step, the meaning of which is clear to all of us. All seven of us know what this means. It means that she is nothing else but a god-damn degenerate! is one way of looking at it, at this complex and difficult question. It means that the 'not-with' is experienced as more pressing, more real, than the 'being-with.' It means she seeks a new lover. *Quelle tragédie!* But the essential loneliness of the person must also be considered. Each of us is like a tiny single hair, hurled into the world among billions and billions of other hairs, of various colors and lengths. And if God does not exist, then we are in even graver shape than we had supposed. In that case, each of us is like a tiny little mote of pointlessness, whirling in the midst of a dreadful free even greater pointlessness, unless there is intelligent life on other planets, that is to say, life even more intelligent than us, life that has thought up some point for this great enterprise, life. That is possible. That is something we do not know, thank God. But in the meantime, here is the hair, with its multiple meanings. What am I to do about it?"

Reaction to the hair (*flashback*): Paul sat in his baff, under the falling water. More hot water fell into the baff. "I would retract the green sea, and the brown fish in it, and I would especially retract that long black hair hanging from that window, that I saw today on my way here, from the Unemployment Office. It has made me terribly nervous, that hair. It was beautiful, I admit it. Long black hair of such texture, fineness, is not easily come by. Hair black as ebony! Yet it has made me terribly nervous. Teeth . . . piano lessons . . ."

EBONY

EQUANIMITY

ASTONISHMENT

TRIUMPH

VAT

DAX

BLAGUE

Lack of reaction to the hair: Dan sat down on a box, and pulled up more boxes for us, without forcing us to sit down on them, but just leaving them there, so that if we wanted to sit down on them, we could. "You know, Klipschorn was right I think when he spoke of the 'blanketing' effect of ordinary language, referring, as I recall, to the part that sort of, you know, 'fills in' between the other parts. That part, the 'filling' you might say, of which the expression 'you might say' is a good example, is to me the most interesting part, and of course it might also be called the 'stuffing' I suppose, and there is probably also, in addition, some other word that would do as well, to describe it, or maybe a number of them. But the quality this 'stuffing' has, that the other parts of verbality do not have, is two-parted, perhaps: (1) an 'endless' quality and (2) a 'sludge' quality. Of course that is possibly two qualities but I prefer to think of them as different aspects of a single quality, if you can think that way. The 'endless' aspect of 'stuffing' is that it goes on and on, in many different forms, and in fact our exchanges are in large measure composed of it, in larger measure even, perhaps, than they are composed of that which is not 'stuffing.' The 'sludge' quality is the *heaviness* that this 'stuff' has, similar to the heavier motor oils, a kind of downward pull but still fluid, if you follow me, and I can't help thinking that this downwardness is valuable, although it's hard to say just how, right at the moment. So, summing up, there is a relation between what I have been saying and what we're doing here at the plant with these plastic buffalo humps. Now you're probably familiar with the fact that the per-capita production of trash in this country is up from 2.75 pounds per day in 1920 to 4.5 pounds per day in 1965, the last year for which we have figures, and is increasing at the rate of about four percent a year. Now that rate will probably go up, because it's *been* going up, and I hazard that we may very well soon reach a point where it's 100 percent. Now at such a point, you will agree, the question turns from a question of disposing of this 'trash' to a question of appreciating its qualities, because, after all, it's 100 percent, right? And there can no longer be any question of 'disposing' of it, because it's all there is, and we will simply have to learn how to 'dig' it—that's slang, but peculiarly appropriate here. So that's why we're in humps, right now, more really from a philosophical point of view than because we find them a great moneymaker. They are 'trash,' and what in fact could be more useless or trashlike? It's that we want to be on the leading edge of this trash phenomenon, the everted sphere of the future, and that's why we pay particular attention, too, to those aspects of language that may be seen as a model of the trash phenomenon. And it's certainly been a pleasure showing you around the plant this afternoon, and meeting you, and talking to you about these things, which are really more important, I believe, than people tend to think. Would you like a cold Coke from the Coke machine now, before you go?"

Additional reactions to the hair: "To be a horse-wife," Edward said. "That, my friends, is my text for today. This important slot in our society, conceptualized by God as very nearly the key to the whole thing as Thomas tells us, has suffered in recent months and in this house a degree of denigration. I have heard it; I have been saddened by it. So I want today if I can to dispel some of these wrong ideas that have been going around, causing confusion and scumming up the face of the truth. *The horsewife!* The very basebone of the American plethora! *The horsewife!* Without whom the entire structure of civilian life would crumble! Without the horsewife, the whole *raison d'être* of our existences would be reduced, in a twinkling, to that brute level of brutality for which we so rightly reproach the filthy animals. Were it not for her enormous purchasing power and the heedless gaiety with which it is exercised, we would still be going around dressed in skins probably, with no big-ticket items to fill the empty voids, in our homes and in our hearts. *The horsewife!* Nut and numen of our intersubjectivity! *The horsewife!* The chiefest ornament on the golden tree of human suffering! But to say what I have said, gentlemen, is to say nothing at all. Consider now the horsewife in another part of her role. Consider her sitting in her baff, anointing her charms with liquid Cheer and powdered Joy which trouble, confuse and drown the sense in odors. Now she rises chastely, and chastely abrades herself with a red towel. What an endearing spectacle! The naked wonder of it! The blue beauty of it! Now I ask you, gentlemen, what do we have here? Do we have a being which regards itself with the proper amount of self-love? No. No, we do not. Do we have a being which regards itself with the appropriate awe? No. No, we do not. We have here rather a being which regards itself, *qua* horsewife, with something dangerously akin to self-hatred. That is the problem. What is the solution." Dan spoke up, then. "I could cut your gizzard out, Edward. You are making the whole damned thing immensely more difficult than it has to be. I put it to you that, without your screen of difficulty-making pseudo-problems, the whole damned thing can be resolved very neatly, in the following way. Now, what do we apprehend when we apprehend Snow White? We apprehend, first, two three-quarter-scale breasts floating toward us wrapped, typically, in a red towel. Or, if we are apprehending her from the other direction, we apprehend a beautiful snow-white arse floating away from us wrapped in a red towel. Now I ask you: What, in these two quite distinct apprehensions, is the constant? The factor that remains the same? Why, quite simply, the red towel. I submit that, rightly understood, the problem of Snow White has to do at its center with nothing else but *red towels*. Seen in this way, it immediately becomes a non-problem. We can easily dispense with the slippery and untrustworthy and expensive effluvia that is Snow White, and cleave instead to the towel. That is my idea, gentlemen. And I have here in this brown bag . . . I have taken the liberty of purchasing . . . here, Edward, here is your towel . . . Kevin . . . Clem. . . . " Chang watched sourly. That was the trouble with being a Chinese. Too much detachment. "I don't want a ratty old red towel. *I want the beautiful snow-white arse itself!*"

SNOW WHITE regarded her hair hanging out of the window. "Paul? Is there a Paul, or have I only projected him in the shape of my longing, boredom, ennui and pain? Have I been trained in the finest graces and arts all my life for nothing but this? Is my richly-appointed body to go down the drain, at twenty-two, in this horribly boresome milieu, which even my worst enemi would not wish upon me, if she knew? Of course there is a Paul! That Paul who was a friend of the family, who had, at that point, not yet assumed the glistering mantle of princeliness. There is a Paul somewhere, but not here. Not under my window. Not yet." Snow White looked out of the window, down the hair, at the two hundred citizens on the ground, agape. "Ugh! I wish I were somewhere else! On the beach at St. Tropez, for example, surrounded by brown boys without a penny. Here everyone has a penny. Here everyone worships the almighty penny. Well at least with pennies one knows what they add up to, under the decimal system. No ambiguity there, at least. O Jerusalem, Jerusalem! Thy daughters are burning with torpor and a sense of immense wasted potential, like one of those pipes you see in the oil fields, burning off the natural gas that it isn't economically rational to ship somewhere!"

"Informal statements   the difficulties of owner-
ship and customs   surprises you by being
Love exchanges   paint it   understanding
brown boys without a penny   I was   bandit
headgear   And the question of yesterday waiting   members   clinging clear milk of wanting
fever hidden   melted constabulary   extra inn-
ings of danger   hides   under the leg résumé
    clip chrome method   decision of the sacred
Rota   muscular dream basket gesture   Kiss
the paper with it   tufts   more interesting than
children   painful texture of interesting children
offensive candor   lesion   hanging mirror
They only want window boxes moving with clean,
careful shrubs   Manner in which the penetration
was   Excited groans stifled under   blankets
upset   A parliament of less-favored glass doors
closed   extra"

THE bishop in his red mantlepiece strode forward. "Yes, we are in a terrible hurricane here," he acknowledged to the wrecked cries of the survivors. "If we can just cross that spit of land there" (gesture with fingers, glitter of episcopal rings) "and get to that harlot over there" (sweep of arm in white lacy alb) "pardon I meant *hamlet*, we can perhaps find shelter against this particular vicissitude sent by God to break our backs for our sins." The "flock" moaned. They had been eight days without . . . The sudden pall on the fourth day had been the worst. There was a silence. Silence. Everything silent. Not a sound for six hours. Nothing. "This is the worst," they murmured to one another in sign language, not wanting to . . . break the. . . . A few young men of good family crawled away into the night to find help (tingle of mace against bone). The Marchesa de G. had fainted again. Blockflutes were heard. "So this is Spain!" Paul said to himself. "I never thought I would live to see it. It is intelligent of me to hide from the Order here, in the episcopal entourage. And it is intelligent of me to hide from the Order here in this hurricane. So much intelligence! So little of God's grace!"

SELF-REGARD is rooted in breakfast. When you have had it, then lunch seems to follow naturally, as if you owned not only the fruits but the means of production in a large, *faux-naïf* country. This is doubted only by eccentrics, and on the present occasion their views need not be taken into account. That country in which you are loved for yourself is expanding now with the further development of books, a new kind capable of satisfying the tactile wishes even of old people. Our engineers are at a loss to understand what their engineers have done. Still, insofar as they are trying to sketch future trends, even the most rigid empiricists among them are obliged to make projections, and then plans. Such is the impact of technology upon the fabric of inherited social institutions that breakfast is almost forgotten, in some countries; they paint pictures instead. I read Dampfboot's novel although he had nothing to say. It wasn't rave, that volume; we regretted that. And it was hard to read, dry, bread-like pages that turned, and then fell, like a car burned by rioters and resting, wrong side up, at the edge of the picture plane with its tires smoking. Fragments kept flying off the screen into the audience, fragments of rain and ethics. Hubert wanted to go back to the dog races. But we made him read his part, the outer part where the author is praised and the price quoted. We like books that have a lot of *dreck* in them, matter which presents itself as not wholly relevant (or indeed, at all relevant) but which, carefully attended to, can supply a kind of "sense" of what is going on. This "sense" is not to be obtained by reading between the lines (for there is nothing there, in those white spaces) but by reading the lines themselves—looking at them and so arriving at a feeling not of satisfaction exactly, that is too much to expect, but of having read them, of having "completed" them. "Please don't talk," Snow White said. "Say nothing. We can begin now. Take off the pajamas." Snow White took off her pajamas. Henry took off his pajamas. Kevin took off his pajamas. Hubert took off his pajamas. Clem took off his pajamas. Dan took off his pajamas. Edward took off his pajamas. Bill refused to take off his pajamas. "Take off your pajamas Bill," Snow White said. Everyone looked at Bill's pajamas. "No, I won't," Bill said. "I will not take off my pajamas." "Take off your pajamas Bill," everyone said. "No. I will not." Everyone looked again at Bill's pajamas. Bill's pajamas filled the room, in a sense. Those yellow crêpe-paper pajamas.

"WHAT is that apelike hand I see reaching into my mailbox?" "That's nothing. Think nothing of it. It's nothing. It's just one of my familiars mother. Don't think about it. It's just an ape that's all. Just an ordinary ape. Don't give it another thought. That's all there is to it." "I think you dismiss these things too easily Jane. I'm sure it means more than that. It's unusual. It means something." "No mother. It doesn't mean more than that. Than I have said it means." "I'm sure it means more than that Jane." "No mother it does not mean more than that. Don't go reading things into things mother. Leave things alone. It means what it means. Content yourself with that mother." "I'm certain it means more than that." "No mother."

SNOW WHITE received the following note from Fred, tossed over the wall:

Madonna,

My men have left me now. They have gone I suspect to the union hall to institute proceedings against me. But I don't care. There is nothing in life for me except being in your power. I have swooned several times this morning, sitting on a bench in the square, thinking of you and feeling those iron bolts with which our souls are bolted together forever. Will you speak to me? I will be in the square at four o'clock by the cathouse clock. Dare I expect, that you will come?

FRED

Hubert picked up the note in the yard. "What is this note doing here, wrapped about a box of Whitman's chocolates? For whom is it intended? After I have read it, I will know." Silently Hubert opened the box of chocolates. "Should I take one of the ones covered with gold foil, always the tastiest? Or should I instead take one of the plain American ones?" Hubert sat down in the yard and looked into the box, trying to make up his mind.

THEN we had a fantasy, a fantasy of anger and malevolence. We were dreaming. We dreamed we burned Snow White. Burned is not the right word, cooked is the right word. We cooked Snow White over the big fire, in the dream. You remember the burning scene in Dreyer's *The Burning of Joan of Art*. It was like that, only where Dreyer was vertical, we were horizontal. Snow White was horizontal. She was spitted on a spit (large iron bar). The spit was suspended over the big fire. Kevin threw more wood on the fire, in the dream. Hubert threw more wood on the fire. Bill threw more wood on the fire. Clem basted the naked girl with sweet-and-sour sauce. Dan made the rice. Snow White screamed. Edward turned the crank which made the meat revolve. Was she done enough? She was making a lot of noise. The meat was moving toward the correct color, a brown-red. The meat thermometer registered almost-enough. "Turn the crank Edward," Bill said. Hubert threw more wood on the fire. Jane threw more wood on the fire. The smoke was acrid, as it always is. Antonin Artaud held out a crucifix at the end of a long pole, in the smoke. Snow White asked if we would remove the spit. "It hurts," she said. "No," Bill said. "You are not done yet. It is supposed to hurt." Jane laughed. "Why are you laughing Jane?" "I am laughing because it is not me burning there." "For you," Henry said, "we have the red-hot iron shoes. The plastic red-hot iron shoes." "This has nothing to do with justice," Bill said. "This has to do with animus." We regarded Snow White rotating there, in her pain and beauty, in the dream.

SNOW WHITE saw her hair black as ebony hanging out of the window. "I suppose I must respond in some way to the new overture from the seven men. They think they are so *merveilleux*, with their new shower curtain. They have been posing in front of it all day. As if I could be swayed, in my iron resolve, by a new shower curtain, however extraordinary and fine! I wonder what it looks like?"

BILL has dropped the money. He was carrying the money neatly separated into 10's, 20's, 50's and so forth, a bundle totaling a great deal of money I can tell you that. He was on his way to the vault with the money bundled into his armpit, wrapped in a red towel. Henry had wrapped it in a red towel. Hubert had bundled it into Bill's armpit. Dan had opened the door. Kevin had pointed Bill toward the vault. Clem had given Bill a kick in the back, to get him started. And Edward had said, "Don't forget the receipt." Then Bill had moved through the door out into the daylight in the direction of the vault. But somewhere between the house and the vault the money hurled itself out of his armpit in a direction known only to it. "Where is the deposit slip, Bill?" Edward asked, when Bill returned. "Deposit slip?" Bill said. "The bundle," Dan said. "The bundle?" "The money," Kevin said. "The money?" We all rushed out into the air, then, to recover the bundle. But it was nowhere. We retraced Bill's steps as best we could. Some of Bill's steps led into a bar & grill, The Fire Next Time Bar & Grill. We retraced there a hot pastrami sandwich and eight bottles of Miller High Life. But of the bundle there was not a trace. Luckily the matter is not serious, because we have more money. But the loss of equanimity was serious. We prize equanimity, and a good deal of equanimity leaked away, that day.

"ALL right Jane get into the car." "Hogo you are making stains on my new white-duck love seat with pillows of white-on-white Indian crewel!" Jane regarded the large black stains. "That's all you know Hogo isn't it. How to take a thing that was white, and stain it until it is black. That's a pretty strong metaphor Hogo of what you would like to do with me, too. I understand. If you think for one moment that your capability of staining the thing you love has escaped me, from the very beginning, you have grossly misperceived our situation. Get out of here Hogo forever!" "All right Jane get into the car."

PAUL was explaining music to the French citizens. "When we turn our amplifiers on," he said, "already cant is forming over some people's minds, like the brown crust on bread, or the silence that 'crusts over' inappropriate remarks. I think there ought to be, and remember I'm talking normatively here, I think what ought to obtain is a measure of *audacity*, an audacity component, such as turning your amplifier up a little higher than anybody else's, or using a fork to pick and strum, rather than a plectrum or the carefully calloused fingertips, or doing something with your elbow, I don't care what, I insist only that it be *relevant*, in a strange way, to the scene that has chosen to spread itself out before us, the theatre of our lives. And if you other gentlemen will come with me down to the quai, carrying your amplifiers in boxes, and not forgetting the trailing cords, which have to be 'plugged in,' so that we can 'turn on' . . ."

ROME. ANOTHER DEFEAT. PAUL HANDS OVER THE GREEN-AND-GOLD ARMBAND. THE ITALIAN POSTAL SERVICE ABIDES NO RINGERS IN ITS RANKS.

WELL Paul is back and he has decided to stop fleeing his destiny and he has given himself up at the Nevada monastery and drawn his robes from the supply room and now he is home on leave in his robes. Paul came to the party in his robes. He wasn't allowed to eat or drink anything, or say anything. That was the Rule. We went to the howling party sitting primly along the side of the room in a row, the seven of us and Snow White. Our social intercourse for the quarter. We discussed the bat theory of child-raising with the mothers there meanwhile paying attention to a vat of rum under the harpsichord. Edward didn't want to discuss the bat theory of child-raising (delicate memories) so he discussed Harald Bluetooth, king of Scandinavia during a certain period, the Bluetooth period. But the mothers wanted to talk. "Spare the bat and the child rots," said the mothers. "Rots inside." "But how do you know when to employ it? The magic moment?" "We have a book which tells us such things," the mothers said. "We look it up in the book. On page 331 begins a twelve-page discussion of batting the baby. A well-worn page." We got away from those mothers as fast as we could. There were a lot of other people talking there, political talk and other kinds of talk. A certain contempt for the institutions of society was exhibited. Clem thrust his arm into the bag of consciousness-expanding drugs. His consciousness expanded. He concentrated his consciousness upon a thumbtip. "Is this the upper extent of knowing, this dermis that I perceive here?" Then he became melancholy, melancholy as a gib cat, melancholy as a jugged hare. "The content of the giraffe is giraffe meat. Giraffes have high blood pressure because the blood must plod to the brain up ten feet of neck." There were more perceptions and *blague*. Edgar and Charles wanted some too. But they were not allowed to have any. All they were allowed to do was hold Paul's robes, when he walked around. "Take me home," Snow White said. "Take me home instantly. If there is anything worse than being home, it is being out."

"YOU shouldn't drop your garbage out of windows Hogo," Jane said. I understood what she was saying. But Hogo is a cruel parody of ultimate concern. His garbage falls on Northerners and Southerners and Westerners alike. "I had a dream," Jane said. "In the dream we were drinking a yellow wine. Then the winemaker came in. He said the wine was made of old copies of the *National Geographic*. I had thought it tasted musty. Then he said no, that was just a joke. The wine was really made of grapes, like every wine. But these were grapes to which the sun had not been kind, he said. They had shriveled for lack of the sun's love. That was why the wine was like that. Then he talked about lovers and husbands. He said the lover eats his meat with his eyes not on the meat but on the eyes of the beloved. The husband watches the meat. The husband knows that the meat will fly away if not watched. The winemaker thought this was really a funny story. He laughed and laughed." Hogo got ready to say something despicable. But it was too late. "That's pretty careless," Hubert said, and we all agreed that if you were going to have a girl tied to a bed, then at least the knots should be secure. I had already gotten the flashlight from its place under the sink, and was working on the brilliant yellow and scarlet and blue bandages. We had hoped to slip into the hospital without being challenged, but the doctor recognized us right away.

HENRY had unlocked the locks on the bar and we were all drinking. It was time for a situation report, we felt. "She still sits there in the window, dangling down her long black hair black as ebony. The crowds have thinned somewhat. Our letters have been returned unopened. The shower-curtain initiative has not produced notable results. She is, I would say, aware of it, but has not reacted either positively or negatively. We have asked an expert in to assess it as to timbre, pitch, mood and key. He should be here tomorrow. To make sure we have got the *right sort* of shower curtain. We have returned the red towels to Bloomingdale's." At this point everybody looked at Dan, who vomited. "Bill's yellow crêpe-paper pajamas have been taken away from him and burned. He ruined that night for all of us, you know that." At this point everybody looked at Bill, who was absent. He was tending the vats. "Bill's new brown monkscloth pajamas, made for him by Paul, should be here next month. The grade of pork ears we are using in the Baby Ding Sam Dew is not capable of meeting U.S. Govt. standards, or indeed, any standards. Our man in Hong Kong assures us however that the next shipment will be superior. Sales nationwide are brisk, brisk, brisk. Texas Instruments is down four points. Control Data is up four points. The pound is weakening. The cow is calving. The cactus wants watering. The new building is abuilding with leases covering 45 percent of the rentable space already in hand. The weather tomorrow, fair and warmer."

"HELLO? Is this Hogo de Bergerac?" "Yes this is Hogo de Bergerac." "Well this is the Internal Revenue Service, Baltimore Office, Broat. We have your letter here in which you offer to inform on Bill, Kevin, Edward, Hubert, Henry, Clem and Dan for 17 percent of the monies collected. We deeply appreciate your getting in touch with us but I must tell you that we pay only eight percent." *"Eight percent!"* "Yes I'm sorry I know that's low as these things go around the world and in previous years we have paid more, but it's standard now and if we paid you 17 percent all the other informers would demand the same. You can imagine." *"Eight percent!"* "Yes, well, but of course there's patriotism involved too isn't there." *"Eight percent! That's damned little for doing such a vile and dishonorable thing, damned little."* "Yes I know but what is the nature of your information? You're aware of course that it's not enough just to allege. You have to be able to provide supportive evidence or at least sufficient material to lead to a strong case and ultimately conviction and/or collection." "Eight percent!" "I might also point out that it is your duty as an American citizen to come forward with this information if you have it." "Eight percent, eight percent." "Did you hear me? I said it was your duty as an American—" "I am not an

American citizen. I am under Panamanian registry. So just forget my duty as an American citizen. Eight percent. No, I don't think I'm talking to you any more. There would be some pleasure in doing the thing just for the pure vileness of it, but there is more pleasure in spitting on your eight percent. Goodbye, Baltimore. Eight percent. Goodnight, Baltimore, and bad cess to you."

STANDING in the rotten bathroom, we regarded the new shower curtain. It had two colors, a red and a yellow. The red the red of red cabbage, the yellow the yellow of yellow beans. It had two figures, a kind of schematic peahen, a kind of schematic vase. These repeated, in the manner of wallpaper. There were eight of us standing there in the rotten bathroom, including the visitor. The visitor who had said that it was the best-looking shower curtain in town. Ho ho. That was a chiller. We had known that it was adequate. We had known that it was nice. We had even known that it was "splendid" more or less. That was the idea, that it be "splendid." But we had not known that it was the best-looking shower curtain in town. That we had not known. We looked at the shower curtain with new eyes, or rather, saw it in a new light, the light of the esthetician's remark. The visitor was an esthetician, a professor of esthetics. Even those of us by no means a minority who considered esthetics the least ballsy of the several areas of inquiry subsumed under the term, philosophical thought, were affected by the esthetician's remark. First because it had as subject something that was ours, there in the rotten bathroom, on little silver rings, and second because the speaker was a professor of esthetics, even if there is nothing in it, esthetics, as is likely.

As we stood there shoulder to shoulder in the rotten bathroom, the eight of us, a sort of hunger arose, to know if it was true, what he had said. Felt I daresay by all of us, including the esthetician. He must be curious sometimes to know if it is true, what he is saying. We swayed, momentarily, there in the rotten bathroom, in the grip of the hunger. A thousand problems flashed through our mind. How could we determine if it was true, what he had said? Our city, the arena of the proposition, is not large but on the other hand not small, in excess of a hundred thousand souls swelter here awaiting the Last Day and God's mercy. A census of shower curtains was possible but to conduct it we would be forced to neglect the vats and that is something we have sworn never to do, neglect the vats. And to conduct it we would be forced to leave the buildings unwashed, and that is something else we have sworn never to do, leave the buildings unwashed. And granting we managed to gain access to the rotten bathrooms of all hundred thousand souls who swelter here, by what standards were the hundred thousand shower curtains hanging there, on little silver rings, to be assessed? A shower-curtain scale could be constructed with the aid of the professor of esthetics, or with the aid of shower-curtain critics recruited from the curtaining journals, if there are such critics and such journals, I do not doubt it. But even with these preliminary accomplishments, empanelment of shower-curtain critics, from far and near, census of shower-curtain-hanging homes, the quarter-finals, the semi-finals, the finals, we would not be out of the woods yet. For would the decision, broadcast over all media, published throughout the land, not be taken as diddled, in view of the fact that the Olympiad was staged by us, backers of the no doubt winning shower curtain? There was another solution: destruction of the esthetician, who had made the original remark. This thought sighed amongst us, seven heads turned as one to regard the eighth, that of the esthetician, sweating in his velvet collar, there in the rotten bathroom. But destruction of the esthetician, however attractive from a human point of view, would not also ensure destruction of his detritus, his remark. The remark would remain in memory, in our memories. We would then be forced to wipe ourselves out also, a step which we would hesitate to take waiting as we are for the Last Day and God's mercy. And how could we be sure after all that he had not made the same remark to someone else, someone not of our circle, some stranger unknown to us? Known to him but unknown to us? And that the remark would not remain unwiped in the brain of this stranger? And how could we be sure that this stranger was not, even as we were standing there, in the rotten bathroom, relaying the remark to some other, even less reputable stranger? And that this second stranger did not have friends, all of an even filthier repute than himself, to whom he intended babbling the remark, at the first opportunity? And that we might not expect a quorum of undesirables, sitting in the cathouse square, to be rubbing and smearing this piece of intelligence with their ruin before six p.m. by the cathouse clock, this very day? We trembled, there in the rotten bathroom, thinking these thoughts.

"I ADMIRE you, Hogo. I admire the way you are what you are, rocklike in your immutability. I also admire the way you use these Pontiac convertible seats for chairs in your house. But mine is uncomfortable. Only because I am glued into it with several pounds of epoxy glue. Oh I know I laughed when you brushed it onto my hips on Wednesday, saying it was honey and I was honey-hipped. I laughed then. But I am not laughing now. Now it has hardened, like your heart toward me, Hogo." "It was honey-colored I said. No more than that. It is because I want you near me Jane for some strange reason I don't even understand myself. It must be atavistic. It must be some dark reason of the blood which the conscious mind does not understand. That is the stinking truth, God's Body but I wish it were not." "Stop it Hogo stop it lest I forget who is the glued party here. Stop it and get me some hot water." The ape-fingers of Jane's familiars penetrated the chain-link-fence walls of Hogo's house. Looking through the walls, past the apes, one could see Jane and Hogo, having a talk. "Hogo this house is an architectural masterpiece in a certain sense." "What sense is that." "In the sense that you get a sense of 'chain' from these chain-like-fence walls that is entirely appropriate to your enterprise. I mean the enterprise of being a bad fellow. And to make the ceiling of General Motors advertising was a brilliant stroke. When one bears in mind that General Motors is Pontiac, and Pontiac is your middle name." "He was an Indian chief Jane, hero of a famous conspiracy, the conspiracy that bears his name in fact." "I know that Hogo. Every schoolboy knows that, and many schoolgirls too, thanks to the democratization of education in our country. How fitting that your ceiling should be named for a . . ." "I thought it fitting." "What is to become of us, Hogo. Of you and me." "Nothing is to become of us Jane. Our becoming is done. We are what we are. Now it is just a question of rocking along with things as they are until we are dead." "You don't paint a very bright picture Hogo." "It's not my picture Jane. I didn't think up this picture that we are confronted with. The original brushwork was not mine. I absolutely separate myself from this picture. I operate within the frame it is true, but the picture—" "How old are you Hogo." "Thirty-five Jane. A not unpleasant age to be." "You don't mind then. That you are not young." "It has its buggy aspects as what does not?" "You don't mind then that you are sagging in the direction of death." "No, Jane."

HUBERT complains that the electric wastebasket has been overheating. I haven't noticed it but that's what Hubert says and Hubert is rarely wrong about things that don't matter. The electric wastebasket is a security item. Papers dropped into it are destroyed instantly. How the electric wastebasket accomplishes this is not known. An intimidation followed by a demoralization eventuating in a disintegration, one assumes. It is not emptied. There are not even ashes. It functions with a quiet hum digesting whatever we do not wish to fall into the hands of the encmi. The record of Bill's trial when he is tried will go into the electric wastebasket. When we considered the destruction of the esthetician we had in mind the electric wastebasket. First dismemberment, then the electric wastebasket. That there are in the world electric wastebaskets is encouraging. Kevin spoke to Hubert. "There is not enough seriousness in what we do," Kevin said. "Everyone wanders around having his own individual perceptions. These, like balls of different colors and shapes and sizes, roll around on the green billiard table of consciousness . . ." Kevin stopped and began again. "Where is the figure in the carpet? Or is it just . . . carpet?" he asked. "Where is—" "You're talking a lot of buffalo hump, you know that," Hubert said. Hubert walked away. Kevin stood there.

"That encounter did not go well. Perhaps I said the wrong thing?" Kevin blushed furiously at the thought that he might have said the wrong thing. Red blushes sat upon his neck. "What could I have done, to make it 'go'? What is this gift that others have, that I do not have, that chokes The Other with love, at the very sight of one?" Kevin's pre-encounter happiness leaked away. He had been happy before the encounter, but after it, he was not. "My God but we are fragile."

SNOW WHITE hung her hair again out of the window. It was longer now. It was about four feet long. She had just washed it too with golden Prell. She was experiencing a degree of anger at male domination of the physical world. "Oh if I could just get my hands on the man who dubbed those electrical connections male and female! He thought he was so worldly. And if I could just get my hands on the man who called that piece of pipe a nipple! He thought he was so urbane. But that didn't prevent them from making a hash of the buffalo problem you'll notice. Where have the buffalo gone? You can go for miles and miles and miles and miles and miles and miles and hundreds of miles without seeing a single one! And that didn't prevent them from letting the railroads grab all the best land! And that didn't prevent them from letting alienation seep in everywhere and cover everything like a big gray electric blanket that doesn't work, after you have pushed the off-on switch to the 'on' position! So don't come around and accuse me of not being serious. Women may not be serious, but at least they're not a damned fool!" Snow White took her head out of the window, and pulled in her long black hair which had been dangling down. "No one has come to climb up. That says it all. This time is the wrong time for me. I am in the wrong time.

There is something wrong with all those people standing there, gaping and gawking. And with all those who did not come and at least *try* to climb up. To fill the role. And with the very world itself, for not being able to supply a prince. For not being able to at least be civilized enough to supply the correct ending to the story."

PART THREE

PART THREE

SNOW WHITE had another glass of healthy orange juice. "From now on I deny myself to them. These delights. I maintain an esthetic distance. No more do I trip girlishly to their bed in the night, or after lunch, or in the misty mid-morning. Not that I ever did. It was always my whim which governed those gregarious encounters summed up so well by Livy in the phrase, *vae victis*. I congratulate myself on that score at least. And no more will I chop their onions, boil their fettucini, or marinate their flank steak. No more will I trudge about the house pursuing stain. No more will I fold their lingerie in neat bundles and stuff it away in the highboy. I am not even going to speak to them, now, except through third parties, or if I have something special to announce—a new nuance of my mood, a new vagary, a new extravagant caprice. I don't know what such a policy will win me. I am not even sure I wish to implement it. It seems small and mean-spirited. I have conflicting ideas. But the main theme that runs through my brain is that what is, is insufficient. Where did that sulky notion come from? From the rental library, doubtless. Perhaps the seven men should have left me in the forest. To perish there, when all the roots and berries and rabbits and robins had been exhausted. If I had perished then, I would not be thinking now. It is true that there is a future in which I shall inevitably perish. There is that. Thinking terminates. One shall not always be leaning on one's elbow in the bed at a quarter to four in the morning, wondering if the Japanese are happier than their piglike Western contemporaries. Another orange juice, with a little vodka in it this time."

"I HAVE killed this whole bottle of Chablis wine by myself," Dan said. "And that other bottle of Chablis too—that one under the bed. And that other bottle of Chablis too—the one with the brown candle stuck in the mouth of it. And I am not afraid. Not of what may come, not of what has been. Now I will light that long cigar, that cigar that stretches from Mont St. Michel and Chartres, to under the volcano. What is merely fashionable will fade away, and what is merely new will fade away, but what will not fade away, is the way I feel: analogies break down, regimes break down, but the way I feel remains. I feel abandoned. After a hard day tending the vats, and washing the buildings, one wants to come home and find a leg of mutton on the table, in a rich gravy, with little pearly onions studded in it, and perhaps a small pot of Irish potatoes somewhere about. Instead I come home to this nothingness. Now she sits in her room reading *Dissent* and admiring her figure in the mirror. She still loves us, in a way, but it isn't enough. It is a failure of leadership, I feel. We have been left sucking the mop again. True leadership would make her love us fiercely and excitingly, as in the old days. True leadership would find a way out of this hairy imbroglio. I am tired of Bill's halting explanations, promises. If he doesn't want to lead, then let us vote. That is all I have to say, except one more thing: when one has been bending over a hot vat all day, one doesn't want to come home and hear a lot of hump from a cow-hearted leader whose leadership buttons have fallen off—some fellow who spends the dreamy days eating cabbage and watching ships, while you are at work. Work, with its charts, its lines of authority, its air of importance."

"THE refusal of emotion produces nervousness," Bill said dipping into the barrel of decadent absinthe. "Remember that. You are tense as a wirewalker, Hubert. If it is still possible to heave a sigh you should heave it. If it is still possible to rip out a groan you should rip it out. If it is still possible to smite the brow with anguished forefinger then you should let that forefinger fall. And there are expostulations and entreaties that meet the case to be found in old books, look them up. This concatenation of outward and visible signs may I say may detonate an inward invisible subjective correlative, booming in the deeps of the gut like an Alka-Seltzer to produce tranquillity. I say may. And you others there, lounging about with expressions of steely unconcern, you are just like Hubert. The disease is the same and the remedy is the same. As for me, I am out of it. I have copted out if you want to put it that way. After a life rich in emotional defeats, I have looked around for other modes of misery, other roads to destruction. Now I limit myself to listening to what people say, and thinking what pamby it is, what they say. My nourishment is refined from the ongoing circus of the mind in motion. Give me the odd linguistic trip, stutter and fall, and I will be content. Actually, when you get right down to it, I should be the monk, and Paul the leader here." "We have entertained the notion," Hubert said.

"THEY can treat me like a rube if they wish," Clem said holding tightly to the two hundred bottles of Lone Star at the Alamo Chili House. "I suppose I am a rubish hayseed in some sense, full of downhome notions that contradict the more sophisticated notions of my colleagues. But I notice that it is to me they come when it is a question of grits or chitlings or fried catfish. Of course these questions do not arise very often. I have not had a whiff of fried catfish these twelve years! How many nights have I trudged home with my face fixed for fried catfish, only to find that we were having fried calimaretti or some other Eastern dish. Not that I would put down those tender rings of squid deep-fried in olive oil. I even like the squarish can the olive oil comes in, emblazoned with green-and-gold devices, flowery emblemature out of the nineteenth century. It makes my mouth water just to look at it, that can. But why am I talking to myself about cans? Cans are not what is troubling me. What is troubling me is the quality of life in our great country, America. It seems to me to be deprived. I don't mean that the deprived people are deprived, although they are, clearly, but that even the fat are deprived. I suppose one could say that they are all humpheads and let it go at that. I am worried by the fact that no one responded to Snow White's hair initiative. Even though I am at the same time relieved. But it suggests that Americans will not or cannot see themselves as princely. Even Paul, that most princely of our contemporaries, did not respond appropriately. Of course it may be that princely is not a good thing to be. And of course there is our long democratic tradition which is anti-aristocratic. Egalitarianism precludes princeliness. And yet our people are not equal in any sense. They are either . . . The poorest of them are slaves as surely as if they were chained to gigantic wooden oars. The richest of them have the faces of cold effete homosexuals. And those in the middle are wonderfully confused. Redistribute the money. That will not ameliorate everything, but it will ameliorate some things. Redistribute the money. This can be achieved in only one way. By making the rich happier. New lovers. New lovers who will make their lives exciting and 'rich' in a way that . . . We must pass a law that all marriages of people with more than enough money are dissolved as of tomorrow. We will free all these poor moneyed people and let them out to play. The quid pro quo is their money. Then we take the money and—"

EDWARD was blowing his mind, under the board-walk. "Well my mind is blown now. Nine mantras and three bottles of insect repellent, under the boardwalk. I shall certainly be sick tomorrow. But it is worth it to have a blown mind. To stop being a filthy bourgeois for a space, even a short space. To gain access to everything in a new way. Under the boardwalk. Those cream Corfam shoes clumping overhead. I understand them now, for the first time. Not their molecular structure, in which I am not particularly interested, but their sacredness. Their centrality. They are the center of everything, those shoes. They are it. I know that, now. Too bad it is not worth knowing. Too bad it is not true. It is not even temporarily true. Well, that must mean that my mind is not fully blown. That harsh critique. More insect repellent!"

IT WAS NOT UNTIL THE 19TH CEN-
TURY THAT RUSSIA PRODUCED A LIT-
ERATURE WORTHY OF BECOMING
PART OF THE WORLD'S CULTURAL
HERITAGE. PUSHKIN DISPLAYED VER-
BAL FACILITY. GOGOL WAS A RE-
FORMER. AS A STYLIST DOSTOEVSKY
HAD MANY SHORTCOMINGS. TOL-
STOY . . .

IN her chamber Snow White removed her coat, and then her shirt, and then her slip, and then her bra. The bare breasts remained. Standing by the window Snow White regarded her bare breasts, by pointing her head down. "Well, what is there to think about them? Usually I don't think about them at all, but think, rather, about common occurrences, like going to the bowling alley or seeing, in the sky, the wingspread of a gigantic jet aircraft. But recent events, or lack of events, have provoked in me a crisis of confidence. But let us take stock. These breasts, my own, still stand delicately away from the trunk, as they are supposed to do. And the trunk itself is not unappealing. In fact *trunk* is a rather mean word for the main part of this assemblage of felicities. The cream-of-wheat belly! The stunning arse, in the rococo mirror! And then the especially good legs, including the important knees. I have nothing but praise for this delicious assortment! But my curly mind has problems distinct from although related to those of my scrumptious body. The curious physicality of my existence here on Earth is related to both parts of the mind-body problem, the mind part and the body part. Although I secretly know that my body *is* my mind. The way it acts sometimes, spontaneously and scandalously hurling itself into the arms of bad situations, with never a care for who is watching or real values. No wonder we who are twenty-two don't trust anybody over twelve. That is where you find people who know the score, under twelve. I think I will go out and speak to some eleven-year-olds, now, to refresh myself. Now or soon." Snow White regarded her nice-looking breasts. "Not the best I've ever seen. But not the worst."

BOBBLE was one of the boys who was there. He had a hair style that, I don't know, some of you may not like, and there were other things wrong with him too. I had thought that in terms of mettle he would glister like a fire escape. Whereas in fact he was a sack of timidities. That much was clear. But we had sent for him so we had to talk to him. "All right lad this is what we want with you. Your mission is this: to go out into the world and pull down all those election posters. We have decided to stop voting, so pull down the posters. Let's get all those ugly faces off our streets and out of our elective offices. We are not going to vote any more, no matter how often they come around with their sound trucks and statesmanlike gestures. Pull down the sound trucks. Pull down the outstretched arms. To hell with the whole business. Voting has turned out to be a damned impertinence. They never do what we want them to do anyhow. And when they do what we don't want them to do, they don't do it well. To hell with them. We are going to save up all our votes for the next twenty years and spend them all at one time. Maybe by that day there will be some Rabelaisian figure worth spending them on. And so, raw youth, with your tentative air, go out and work our will on the physical world. We are going to go whole hog on this program, to a certain extent, and you are our chosen instrument. We are not particularly proud of you, but you exist, in some rough way, and that is enough, for our purposes. You are sub-attractive, Bobble, and so are your peers there, but here is the money, and there is the task. Get going."

UNDER the tree, Paul stood looking through the window at Snow White, with her bare breasts. "God Almighty," Paul said to himself. "It's a good thing it occurred to me to stand under this tree and look through this window. It's a good thing I am on leave from the monastery. It's a good thing I had my reading glasses in my upper robe pocket." Paul read the message written on Snow White's unwrapped breasts. "She is just like one of those dancers one sees from time to time on Bourbon Street in New Orleans, and in selected areas of other cities. In the smaller cities the dancers are sometimes forced by the police to put on more garb. But without garb, these girls bring joy, with their movements, lack of movements. . . . Dancing is diverting if you are watching, and also if you are dancing yourself. But how can you 'dance yourself'? Is 'self-dancing' the answer? I was fond of stick dancing at one time. There was some joy in that. But then a man came and said I was using the wrong kind of stick. He was a stick-dancing critic, he said, and no one used that kind of stick any more. The stick of choice, he said, was more brutal than the one I was using, or less brutal, I forget which. Brutalism had something to do with it. I said, fuck off, buddy, leave me alone with my old stick, the stick of my youth. He fucked off, then.

But I became dissatisfied with that stick, subjected as it had been for the first time to the scrutiny of a first-rate intelligence. I sublet the stick. And that is why I have become everything I have become since, including what I now am, a voyeur." Paul looked again at the upper part of Snow White. "Looking through this window is sweet. The sweetest thing that has happened to me in all my days. Sweet, sweet." Paul savored the sweetness of human communication, through the window.

PAUL HAS NEVER BEFORE REALLY

SEEN SNOW WHITE AS A WOMAN.

HOGO pushed Paul away from the bloody tree. "You are a slime sir, looking through that open window at that apparently naked girl there, the most beautiful and attractive I have ever seen, in all my life. You are a dishonor to the robes you wear. That you stand here without shame gazing at that incredible beauty, at her snowy buttocks and so forth, at that natural majesty I perceive so well, through the window, is endlessly reprehensible, in our society. I have seen some vileness in my time, but your action in spying upon this beautiful unknown beauty, whom I already love with all my heart until the end of time, is the most vile thing that the mind of man ever broached. I am going to set a rat chewing at your anus, false monk, for if there is anything this world affords, it is punishment." "You have a good line, fellow," Paul said coolly. "Perhaps next you would care to make a few remarks about unearned pessimism as original sin." "It is true that I am generally in favor of earned pessimism, Paul," Hogo said. "And I have earned mine. Yet at the same time I seem to feel a new vigor, optimism and hope, simply through the medium of pouring my eyes through this window." "It is strong medicine, this," Paul said, and they put their arms around each other's shoulders to look some more, but Hogo was thinking about how he could get rid of Paul, once and for all, permanently.

HOGO began to make a plan. It was to be a large plan, a plan as big as a map. Make no small plans, as Pott has said. The object of the plan was to get inside the house when no one was there. No one but Snow White. Hogo played Polish music on his player. Then he stuck pins in his plan marking points of entry and points of ejection. Pins of red, blue, violet, green, yellow, black and white bespattered the plan. The plan oozed out over the floor of the living room into the dining room. Then it ran into the kitchen, bedroom and hall. Plant life from the bursting nature outside came to regard the plan. A green finger of plant life lay down on top of the plan. Jane entered trailing a shopping cart filled with shopping. "What is all this paper on the floor?" Hogo lay atop the plan, and atop the plant life, attempting to conceal them. "It's nothing. Some work I brought home from the office." "Why then are you making those swimming motions on top of it?" "I was taking a nap." "It doesn't look like a nap to me." Hogo regarded Jane. He noticed that she had her graceful cello shape, still. "This cello-shaped girl still has some life in her," Hogo reflected. "Why don't I spend more time looking at her and drinking in her seasoned beauty." But then he thought of the viola da gamba-shaped Snow White. "Why is it that we always require 'more,'"

Hogo wondered. "Why is it that we can never be satisfied. It is almost as if we were designed that way. As if that were part of the cosmic design." Hogo gathered up the plan and packed it away in the special planning humidor, constructed especially to keep the plan fresh and exciting. "Maybe I should make cigar wrappers of this plan, to conceal it from its enemies. The cigars to be smoked in a particular order, and in the clouds of smoke arising, the first faint dim blue outlines of the plan. I wonder what the chemistry and physics of that would be." Hogo regarded the packed plan, in its humidor. "It seems to have weak spots. The possibility of resistance from those within." Hogo imagined the resistance leader in his black turtleneck sweater. "I'll wager I never get into that house clandestinely, the resistance will be so stiff. For people who have a treasure, guard it with their lives. What a wonk I am, planning-wise! I will have to think up a new abnegation to punish myself for thinking up a plan this poor—playing the accordion, possibly." "What are you thinking about?" Jane asked holding tensely to the handle of the shopping cart. "Playing the accordion," Hogo said.

THERE was no place for our anger and frustration to go, then, so we went out and hit a dog. It was a big dog, so it was all right. It was fair. The gargantuan iron dog nineteen feet high commemorating the one hundredth anniversary of the invention of meat . . . "Have a care," Kevin said. It was a brisk day, more brisk than some of the others we've had. The girls were wrapping their heads in cloths again, bright-colored cotton going around the top and the back part and tied at the bottom of the back part, where the sweet neck begins. A few derelicts and bums were lying around in front of the house, staining the sidewalk pretty well. Bill looked tired. I gave his face some additional looks. Then some other people came up and said they were actors. "What sort of actors?" "Do you mean good or bad?" "I didn't mean that but what is the answer?" "Bad, I'm afraid," the chief actor said, and we turned away. That wasn't what we'd wanted to hear. Everything was complex and netlike. The stain was still there filtering through the water supply and the pipes and carried in suitcases too. The old waiter's brown suit had ponyskin lapels. That was depressing. Hogo has announced that Paul is standing in the middle of his, Hogo's, *Lebensraum*. That has an ominous sound. I don't like the sound of that at all. We had a few more Laughing Marys and radishes.

Hogo was sharpening his kris. The whirling grindstone ground the steel. There was a noise, you know it perhaps. Hogo tested the kris against his thumb. A red drop of blood. The kris was functioning correctly. After Hogo finished sharpening his kris he began sharpening his bolo. Then he sharpened his parang and his machete and his dirk. "I like to keep everything sharp."

THE President looked out of his window again. It was another night like that night we described previously and he was looking out of the same window. The Dow-Jones index was still falling. The folk were still in tatters. The President turned his mind for a millisecond to us, here. "Great balls of river mud," the President said. "Is *nothing* going to go right?" I don't blame him for feeling that way. Everything is falling apart. A lot of things are happening. "I love her, Jane," Hogo said. "Whoever she is, she is mine, and I am hers, virtually if not actually, forever. I feel I have to tell you this, because after all I do owe you something for having been the butt of my unpleasantness for so long. For these years." "The poet must be reassured and threatened," Henry said. "In the same way, Bill must be brought to justice for his bungling. This latest bit is the last straw absolutely. I see the trial as a kind of analysis really, more a therapeutic than a judicial procedure. We must discover the reason, for what he did. When he threw those two six-packs of Miller High Life through the windscreen of that blue Volkswagen—" Paul inspected Snow White's window from his underground installation. "A lucky hit! the idea of installing this underground installation not far from the house. Now I can keep her under constant surveillance, through this system of mirrors and trained dogs. One of my trained dogs is even now investigating that overly handsome delivery boy from the meat market, who lingered far too long at the door. I should have a complete report by first light. My God but I had to spend a lot of money on their training. An estimated two thousand dollars per dog. Well, one assumes that it is money well spent. If I undertook this project with undertrained dogs, there is a good chance that everything would go glimmering. Now at least I can rely on the dog aspect of things." Snow White was in the kitchen, scoring the meat. "Oh why does fate give us alternatives to annoy and frustrate ourselves with? Why for instance do I have the option of going out of the house, through the window, and sleeping with Paul in his pit? Luckily that alternative is not a very attractive one. Paul's princeliness has somehow fallen away, and the naked Paul, without his aura, is just another complacent bourgeois. And I thought I saw, over his shoulder, a dark and vilely compelling figure not known to me, as I looked out of my window, in the mirror. Who is that? Compared to that unknown figure, the figure of Paul is about as attractive as a mustard plaster. I would never go to his pit, now. Still, as a possible move, it clutters up the board, obscuring perhaps a more exciting one."

"NOW I have been left sucking the mop again," Jane blurted out in the rare-poison room of her mother's magnificent duplex apartment on a tree-lined street in a desirable location. "I have been left sucking the mop in a big way. Hogo de Bergerac no longer holds me in the highest esteem. His highest esteem has shifted to another, and now he holds her in it, and I am alone with my malice at last. Face to face with it. For the first time in my history, I have no lover to temper my malice with healing balsam-scented older love. Now there is nothing but malice." Jane regarded the floor-to-ceiling Early American spice racks with their neatly labeled jars of various sorts of bane including dayshade, scumlock, hyoscine, azote, hurtwort and milkleg. "Now I must witch someone, for that is my role, and to flee one's role, as Gimbal tells us, is in the final analysis bootless. But the question is, what form shall my malice take, on this occasion? This braw February day? Something in the area of inter-personal relations would be interesting. Whose interpersonal relations shall I poison, with the tasteful savagery of my abundant imagination and talent for concoction? I think I will go around to Snow White's house, where she cohabits with the seven men in a mocksome travesty of approved behavior, and see what is stirring there. If something is stirring, perhaps I can arrange a sleep for it—in the corner of a churchyard, for example."

158

"BILL will you begin. By telling the court in your own words how you first conceived and then supported this chimera, the illusion of your potential greatness. By means of which you have managed to assume the leadership and retain it, despite tons of evidence of total incompetence, the most recent instance being your hurlment of two six-packs of Miller High Life, in a brown-paper bag, through the windscreen of a blue Volkswagen operated by I. Fondue and H. Maeght. Two utter and absolute strangers, so far as we know." "Strangers to you perhaps. But not to me." "Well strangers is not the immediate question. Will you respond to the immediate question. How did you first conceive and then sustain—" "The conception I have explained more or less. I wanted to make, of my life, a powerful statement etc. etc. How this wrinkle was first planted in my sensorium I know not. But I can tell you how it is sustained." "How." "I tell myself things." "What." "Bill you are the greatest. Bill you did that very nicely. Bill there is something about you. Bill you have style. Bill you are *macho*." "But despite this blizzard of self-gratulation—" "A fear remained." "A fear of?" "The black horse." "Who is this black horse." "I have not yet met it. It was described to me." "By?" "Fondue and Maeght." "Those two who were at the controls of the Volkswagen when you hurled the brown-paper bag." "That is correct." "You cherished then for these two, Fondue and Maeght, a hate." "More of a miff, your worship." "Of what standing, in the time dimension, is this miff?" "Matter of let's see sixteen years I would say." "The miff had its genesis in mentionment to you by them of the great black horse." "That is correct." "How old were you exactly. At that time." "Twelve years." "Something said to you about a horse sixteen years ago triggered, then, the hurlment." "That is correct." "Let us make sure we understand the circumstances of the hurlment. Can you disbosom yourself very briefly of the event as seen from your point of view." "It was about four o'clock in the afternoon." "What is your authority." "The cathouse clock." "Proceed." "I was on my way from the coin-operated laundry to the Door Store." "With what in view." "I had in mind the purchasement of a slab of massif oak, 48" by 60", and a set of carved Byzantine legs, for the construction of a cocktail table, to support cocktails." "Could you describe the relation of the High Life to the project, construction of cocktail table." "I had in mind engorgement of the High Life whilst sanding, screwing, gluing and so forth." "And what had you in mind further. The court is interested in the array or disarray of your mind." "I had in mind the making of a burgoo, for my supper. Snow White as you know being reluctant in these days to—" "As we know. There was, then, in the brown-paper bag, material—" "There was in the brown-paper bag, along with the High Life, a flatfish." "The flatfish perished in the hurlment we take it." "The flatfish had perished some time previously. Murthered on the altar of commerce, according to the best information available." "Proceed." "I then apprehended, at the corner of Eleventh and Meat, the blue Volkswagen containing Fondue and Maeght." "You descried them through the windscreen." "That is correct." "The windscreen was in motion?" "The entire vehicle." "Making what speed." "It was effecting a stop." "You were crossing in front of it." "That is correct." "What then." "I recognized at the controls, Fondue and Maeght." "This after the slipping away of sixteen years." "The impression was indelible." "What then." "I lifted my eyes." "To heaven?" "To the cathouse clock. It registered hard upon four." "What then." "The hurlment." "You hurled said bag through said windscreen." "Yes." "And?" "The windscreen shattered. Ha ha." "Did the court hear you aright. Did you say ha ha." "Ha ha." "Outburst will be dealt with. You have been warned. Let us continue. The windscreen glass was then imploded upon the passengers." "Ha ha." "Cutaneous injurement resulted in facial areas a b c and d." "That is correct. Ha ha." "Fondue sustained a woundment in the vicinity of the inner canthus." "That is correct." "Could you locate that for the court." "The junction of the upper and lower lids, on the inside." " 'Inside' meaning, we assume, the most noseward part." "Exactly." "A hair from which, the ball itself would have been compromised." "Fatally." "You then danced a jig on—" "*Objection!*" "And what might the objection be?" "Our client, your honesties, did not *dance a jig*. A certain shufflement of the feet might have been observed, product of a perfectly plausible nervous tension, such as all are subject to on special occasions, weddings, births, deaths, etc. But nothing that, in all charity, might be described as *a gigue,* with its connotations of gaiety, carefreeness—" "He was observed dancing a jig by Shield 333, midst the broken glass and blood." "Could we have Shield 333." "*Shield 333 to the stand!*" "Come along, fellow, come along. Do you swear to tell the truth, or some of it, or most of it, so long as we both may live?" "I do." "Now then, Shield 333, you are Shield 333?" "I are." "It was you who was officiating at the corner of Eleventh and Meat, on the night of January sixteeth?" "It were." "And your mission?" "Prevention of enmanglement of schoolchildren by galloping pantechnicons." "And the weather?" "There was you might say a mizzle. I was wearing me plastic cap cover." "Did you observe that man over there, known as 'Bill,' dancing a jig midst the blood and glass, after the hurlment?" "Well now, I'm nae sae gud on th' dances, yer amplitude. I'm not sure it were a jig. Coulda been a jag. Coulda been what do they call it, th' lap. Hae coulda been lappin'. I'm nae dancer meself. Hem from the Tenth Precinct. Th' Tenth don't dance." "Thank you, Shield 333, for this inconclusive evidence of the worst sort. You may step down. Now, 'Bill,' to return to your entanglement of former times with Fondue and Maeght, in what relation to you did they stand, in those times." "They stood to me in the relation, scoutmasters." "They were your scoutmasters. Entrusted with your schoolment in certain dimensions of lore." "Yes. The duty of the scoutmasters was to reveal the scoutmysteries." "And what was the nature of the latter?" "The scoutmysteries included such things as the mystique of rope, the mistake of one animal for another, and the miseries of the open air." "Yes. Now, was this matter of the great black horse included under the rubric, scoutmysteries." "No. It was in the nature of a threat, a punishment. I had infracted a rule." "What rule?" "A rule of thumb having to do with pots. You were supposed to scour the pots with mud, to clean them. I used Ajax." "That was a scoutmystery, how to scour a pot with mud?" "Indeed." "The infraction was then, resistance to scoutmysteries?" "Stated in the most general terms, that would be it." "And what was the response of Fondue and Maeght." "They told me that there was a great black horse, and that it had in mind, eating me." "They did?" "It would come by night, they said. I lay awake waiting." "Did it present itself? The horse?" "No. But I awaited it. I await it still." "One more question: is it true that you allowed the fires under the vats to go out, on the night of January sixteenth, while pursuing this private vendetta?" "It is true." "Vatricide. That crime of crimes. Well it doesn't look good for you, Bill. It doesn't look *at all* good for you."

SNOW WHITE THINKS: THE HOUSE
. . . WALLS . . . WHEN HE DOESN'T
. . . I'M NOT . . . IN THE DARK
. . . SHOULDERS . . . AFRAID . . .
THE WATER WAS COLD . . . WANT
TO KNOW . . . EFFORTLESSLY . . .

SNOW WHITE THINKS: WHY AM I . . . GLASS . . . HUNCHED AGAINST THE WALL . . . INTELLIGENCE . . . TO RETURN . . . A WALL . . . INTELLIGENCE . . . ON THE . . . TO RETURN . . . HE'S COLD . . . MIRROR . . .

"YOU have to learn to spell everything right," Paul told Emily. "That is the first thing I found intolerable, in other countries. Who can spell *Jeg føler mig daarligt tilpas?* And all it means is *I feel bad,* and I already know that. That I feel bad. If it had meant, for example, *The jug is folded under the darling tulips . . .*" "I understand," Emily said, but she didn't, because she was an animal. Not human. Her problems are not our problems. Forget her. "I try to be reasonable," Paul said, "civil with the telephone company, brusque with the bank. That is what they have earned, that bank, brusqueness, and they can send me all the zinnia seeds in the world and I won't change my opinion. But now that I am a part of the Abbey of Thélème, under the thumb of our fat abbot, I do what I will. That jolly rogue and thin pedant is drunk again, and does not know that I am here, at the catseller's war, earning a penny as a correspondent for *Cat World.* Too bad Snow White is not here with me. It would be good for her, and good for me, and we could crawl behind that pile of used arquebus wads over there and tell each other what we are really like. I already know what I am really like, but I don't know what she is really like. She is probably really like no other girl I have ever known—unlike Joan, unlike Letitia, unlike Mary, unlike Amelia. Unlike those old girls, with whom I spent parts of my youth, the parts that I left with all those priests, in all those dark boxes, with little curtains and sliding doors, before I threw in with the Thélèmites, and began to do what I would. In all sincerity, I am not sure that I am better now than I was then, in those old days. At least then I did not know what I was doing. Now, I know."

"PAUL is frog. He is frog through and through. I thought he would, at some point, cast off his mottled wettish green-and-brown integument to reappear washed in the hundred glistering hues of princeliness. But he is *pure frog*. So. I am disappointed. Either I have overestimated Paul, or I have overestimated history. In either case I have made a serious error. So. There it is. I have been disappointed, and am, doubtless, to be disappointed further. Total disappointment. That's it. The red meat on the rug. The frog's legs on the floor."

"I LOVE YOU, Snow White." "I know, Hogo. I know because you have told me a thousand times. I do not doubt you. I am convinced of your sincerity and warmth. And I must admit that your tall brutality has made its impression on me, too. I am not unaffected by your Prussian presence, or by the chromed chains you wear looped around your motorcycle doublet, or by your tasteful scars on the left and right cheeks. But this 'love' must not be, because of your blood. You don't have the blood for this 'love,' Hogo. Your blood is not fine enough. Oh I know that in this democratic era questions of blood are a little *de trop*, a little frowned-upon. People don't like to hear people talking about their blood, or about other people's blood. But I am not 'people,' Hogo. I am me. I must hold myself in reserve for a prince or prince-figure, someone like Paul. I know that Paul has not looked terribly good up to now and in fact I despise him utterly. Yet he has the blood of kings and queens and cardinals in his veins, Hogo. He has the purple blood of exalted station. Whereas you have only plain blood in your veins, Hogo, blood that anybody might have, the delivery boy from the towel service for example. You must admit that they are not the same thing, these two kinds of blood." "But what about love? What about love which, as Stendhal tells us, seizes the senses and overthrows all other considerations in a giddy of irresponsibility?" "You may well say 'a giddy of irresponsibility,' Hogo. That is precisely the state I am not in. I am calm. As calm as a lamp, as calm as the Secretary of State. As calm as you are giddy." "Well Snow White your blood arguments are pretty potent, and I recognize that there is a gap there, between my blood and the blood royal. Yet in my blood there is a fever. I offer you this fever. It is as if my blood were full of St. Elmo's fire, so hot and electrical does it feel, inside me. If this fever, this rude but grand passion, in any measure ennobles me in your eyes, or in any other part of you, then perhaps all is not yet lost. For even a bad man can set his eyes on the stars, sometimes. Even a bad man can breathe and hope. And it is my hope that, as soon as you fully comprehend the strength of this fever in me, you will find it ennobling and me ennobled, and a fit consort suddenly, though I was not before. I know that this is a slim hope." "No Hogo. It does not ennoble you, the fever. I wish it did, but it does not. It is simply a fever, in my view. Two aspirin and a glass of water. I know that this is commonplace, even cruel, advice, but I have no other advice. I myself am so buffeted about by recent events, and non-events, that if events give me even one more buffet, I will simply explode. Goodnight, Hogo. Take your dark appeal away. Your cunningly-wrought dark appeal."

WE were sitting at a sidewalk café talking about the old days. The days before. Then the proprietor came. He had a policeman with him. A policeman wearing a black leather blackjack and a book by Rafael Sabatini. "You are too far out on the sidewalk," the policeman said. "You must stay behind the potted plants. You must not be more than ten feet from the building line." We moved back behind the building line then. We could talk about the old days on either side of the potted plants, we decided. We were friendly and accommodating, as is our wont. But in moving the table we spilled the drinks. "There will be an additional charge for the stained tablecloth," the proprietor said. Then we poured the rest of the drinks over the rest of the tablecloth, until it was all the same color, rose-red. "Show us the stain," we said. "Where is the stain? Show us the stain and we will pay. And while you are looking for it, more drinks." We looked fondly back over the inches to where we had been. The policeman looked back over the inches with us. "I realize it was better there," the policeman said. "But the law is the law. That is what is wrong with it, that it is the law. You don't mind if I have just a taste of your stain?" The policeman wrung out our tablecover and tossed it off with a flourish of brass. "That's good stain. And now, if you will excuse me, I intuit a felony, over on Pleat Street." The policeman flew away to attend to his felony, the proprietor returned with more stain. "Who has wrinkled my tablecover?" We regarded the tablecover, a distressed area it was true. "Someone will pay for the ironing of that." Then we rose up and wrinkled the entire sidewalk café, with our bare hands. It was impossible to tell who was wrong, when we had finished.

JANE gave Snow White a vodka Gibson on the rocks. "Drink this," she said. "It will make you feel better." "I don't feel bad physically," Snow White said. "Emotionally is another story of course." "Go on," Jane said. "Go on drink it." "No I won't drink it now," Snow White said. "Perhaps later. Although something warns me not to drink it at all. Something suggests to me that it is a bad scene, this drink you proffer. Something whispers to me that there is something wrong with it." "Well that's possible," Jane replied. "I didn't make the vodka myself you know. I didn't grow the grain myself, and reap it myself, and make the mash myself. I am not a member of the Cinzano Vermouth Company. They don't tell me everything. I didn't harvest the onions. I didn't purify the water that went into these rocks. I'm not responsible for everything. All I can say is that to the best of my knowledge, this is an ordinary vodka Gibson on the rocks. Just like any other. Further than that I will not go." "Oh well then," Snow White said. "It must be all right in that case. It must be all right if it is ordinary. If it is as ordinary as you say. In that case, I shall drink it." "This drink is vaguely exciting, like a film by Leopoldo Torre Nilsson," Paul said. "It is a good thing I have taken it away from you, Snow White. It is too exciting for you. If you had drunk it, something bad would probably have happened to your stomach. But because I am a man, and because men have strong stomachs for the business of life, and the pleasure of life too, nothing will happen to me. Lucky that I sensed you about to drink it, and sensed that it was too exciting for you, on my sensing machine in my underground installation, and was able to arrive in time to wrest it from your grasp, just as it was about to touch your lips. Those lips that I have deeply admired, first through the window, and then from my underground installation. Those lips that—" "Look how he has fallen to the ground Jane!" Snow White observed. "And look at all that green foam coming out of his face! And look at those convulsions he is having! Why it resembles nothing else but a death agony, the whole scene! I wonder if there was something wrong with that drink after all? Jane? Jane?"

"ONE thing you can say about him," Fred said, "is that Paul was straight. A straight arrow. And just by looking at him, on those occasions when our paths crossed, at the bus station for instance, or at the discount store, I could tell that Paul had a lot of ginger. He must have had a lot of ginger, to have dug that great hole, outside the house, and to have put all those wires in it, and connected all those dogs to the wires, and all that. That took a lot of mechanical ingenuity, to my way of thinking, and a lot of technical knowledge too, that shouldn't be understated, when we are making our final assessment of Paul. I might mention the trust that Hogo placed in him, as evidenced by the large sum of money found on him, wrapped in one of Hogo's bank statements, when they changed his clothes, at the funeral parlor. Of course some people say that this was get-out-of-town money Hogo had given him, but I don't believe that. I choose to believe that Hogo placed a great deal of trust in Paul, more trust perhaps than the best judgment would suggest, strictly speaking. But I'm talking like a banker now, in a shrill and judicious way, and I don't want to talk like that. Consider Amelia, who is sitting here in the front row with a black cloth over her face, waiting to see her late lover tucked away under the earth, in the box that has been prepared for him.

Imagine one's feelings at such a moment. No, it is too difficult. I shall not ask you to imagine them. I only ask that you empathize with this poor woman, who has been deprived, at a stroke of the Lord's pen as it were, of a source of income and warmth and human intercourse, which we all regard so highly, and need so much. I leave that thought to stick in your minds. As for myself, I am only Fred, a former bandleader spitted on a passion for Snow White, that girl in the third row there, seated next to Jane. She will not even speak to me, even though I am in her power. It seems that being in someone's power implies no obligation on the part of the one in whose power one is, not even the obligation of sparing one a word now and then, or a yellow half-smile. But that is my business, and not the business we are gathered together here in the sight of God to execute, which is the burning of Paul, and the putting of him into a vase, and the sinking of the vase into the ground, in the box that has been prepared for it. Some people like to be scattered on top, but Paul wanted to be put under the ground. That accords with what else we knew about him."

**ANATHEMATIZATION OF THE WORLD
IS NOT AN ADEQUATE RESPONSE TO
THE WORLD.**

TRYING to break out of this bag that we are in. What gave us the idea that there was something better? How does the concept, "something better," arise? What does it look like, this *something better?* Don't tell me that it is an infant's idea because I refuse to believe that. I know some sentient infants but they are not that sentient. And then the great horde of persons sub-sentient who nevertheless can conceive of *something better*. I am thinking of a happy island. Intestate Bill moved toward his lack of reward. We have raised him to the sky. Bill will become doubtless one of those skyheroes, like Theodicy and Rime, who govern the orderly rush of virgins and widows through the world. We lifted him toward the sky. Bill will become doubtless one of those sub-deities who govern the calm passage of cemeteries through the sky. If the graves fall open in mid-passage and swathed forms fall out, it will be his fault, probably.

BILL has been hanged. We regret that. He is the first of us ever to be hanged. We regret it. But that was the verdict. We had a hard time hanging him. We had never hanged anyone before. But fortunately we had Hogo to help us. Bill was hanged because he was guilty, and if you are guilty, then you must be hanged. He was guilty of vatricide and failure. He leaped about on the platform quite a bit. It was evident that he didn't wish to be hanged. It was a fearsome amount of trouble, the whole thing. But luckily Hogo was there with his quirt. That expedited things. Now there is a certain degree of equanimity. We prize equanimity. It means things are going well. Bill's friend Dan is the new leader. We have decided to let Hogo live in the house. He is a brute perhaps but an efficient brute. He is good at tending the vats. Dan has taken charge with a fine aggressiveness. He has added three new varieties to the line: Baby Water Chestnuts, Baby Kimchi, Baby Bean Thread. They are moving well, these new varieties. Snow White continues to cast chrysanthemums on Paul's grave, although there is nothing in it for her, that grave. I think she realizes that. But she was fond of his blood, while he was alive. She was fond not of him but of the abstract notion that, to her, meant "him." I am not sure that that is the best idea.

THE FAILURE OF SNOW WHITE'S ARSE

REVIRGINIZATION OF SNOW WHITE

APOTHEOSIS OF SNOW WHITE

SNOW WHITE RISES INTO THE SKY

THE HEROES DEPART IN SEARCH OF

A NEW PRINCIPLE

HEIGH-HO

Donald Barthelme lives in New York City, where he is currently at work on a novel.

His previous books include UNSPEAK-ABLE PRACTICES, UNNATURAL ACTS; CITY LIFE; *and* COME BACK, DR. CALIGARI.

Mr. Barthelme's children's book, THE SLIGHTLY IRREGULAR FIRE ENGINE, OR THE HITHERING THITHERING DJINN, *won a National Book Award in 1972.*